For Not Finding You

Also by Robert Day

The Last Cattle Drive
Speaking French in Kansas and Other Stories
Chance Encounters of a Literary Kind
The Four Wheel Drive Quartet
Where I Am Now
The ABCs of Enlightenment
The Billion Dollar Dream
Robert Day for President
The Committee to Save the World
The Collected Short Stories
Talk to Strangers and Stop on By
We Should Have Come by Water (Poems)
Let Us Now Praise Famous Love (Forthcoming)

For Lauren

ROBERT DAY

For Not Finding You

X

CHESTER RIVER PRESS

2021

This Book is Dedicated to:

Fred Whitehead, Robert Stewart, Michael Malone,
Walton Beacham, Crosby Kemper, Leo Oliva, Meredith Davis Hadaway,
Perry Schwartz, John Harris, Jane Alix, Dan Premo, and Denise Low.

&

Anthony Burgess (February 25, 1917 – November 22, 1993)
Richard Harwood (March 29, 1925 – March 19, 2001)
Walter Bernstein (August 20, 1919 – January 23, 2021)

And for
Kathryn Jankus Day

Paris

I have come to Paris in search of lost love. Many have done it. I live in a small apartment on Rue de Poitiers just behind the Musée d'Orsay that I share with a character from a short story I recently wrote. In spite of who we are to one another, there is room enough for both of us. Monique's collection of Montaigne's selected essays (in both French and English, with her admonishment inscribed on the flyleaf—*traduit par Montaigne tout seul*), is on the desk where I am now typing—along with her French/English *Larousse Dictionary*, inscribed: *For the first time you see Paris. With me!* I have bought my own *Plan de Paris*.

It is fall here. The Bateau Bus is still on the Seine, dropping passengers at various stops: Eiffel Tower, Saint-Germain-des-Prés, Notre Dame, Hôtel de Ville, among others. I am up high enough to watch its wake. I can see the Pont des Arts. I have Monique's postcard.

By now I have lived here a year. (My fictional doppelgänger has been here a month or so. In this way he has moved in on me.) I do not know what has kept me from what I am now writing, nor did I know I was being kept from it. *For Not Finding You* is my provisional title; I hope that will change. I walk a lot to make that possible. Like my character, I am keeping a diary.

ж

West Jesus Land, Kansas

I once worked on a small ranch north of Hays, Kansas, in Buckeye Township—above the Saline River and the breaks that run into it. Some days I taught school as a substitute. I lived in that country six years before I left for Paris. I did not marry.

One Friday, toward the end of summer, the rancher got a call from the banker who had loaned him money to buy the heifers. We had hopes of breeding them and selling the calves for a fat profit. But the price of money was going higher, and the price of beef was going lower. That's when the phone rang. I told the banker that the owner was outside but I would get him.

I will use Buck for his name, but that was not his name. I am superstitious about some things, and writing about the dead and using their names is one of them.

"Hello," Buck said when he got on the phone. He had been walking toward the Home-House when I called him. Long, even strides. He was a tall man with big hands. The phone vanished in his fist. He listened and frowned.

"I don't have that kind of money unless I sell the herd, which I won't," he said. "They're just bred. And the price is piss-poor."

He was shaking his head back and forth. That usually meant he was about to swear. He was gifted at it, and the more he shook his head before he got started, the richer the gift—and the better it gave.

"Tell those pig fuckers on your board that's what they get for lending money at fourteen percent." Hanging up, he said: "You guys are lower than snake shit at the bottom of a posthole."

It wasn't funny, but later that night when we poured ourselves Black Jack it got us laughing as we retold the story more than once, back and forth, adding something with each version. Not about bankers being lower than snake shit at the bottom of a posthole; that was for real.

There were just the two of us working the place in those days. The ranch had been in Buck's family for three generations; however, Buck and his wife, Ellen (also not her real name), had lived most of their lives in Hays. When their hired man died they sold the Hays house and moved to the ranch. And I was to move out from my apartment in Gorham to be with them, living in a small

Sears and Roebuck cabin that I was fixing up to the north of the larger Home-House. But then Ellen died in a crash with a grain truck on the Seven Hills Road from the ranch to Hays. I was still in Gorham when it happened. It took me the fall to fix up the cabin and then I moved in and began helping Buck more or less full time.

The following spring Monique started coming out. We had known each other at the university but got separated the way you do when you are young: she went on a student exchange to France; I took a job teaching school in Gorham. Before we found each other again there had been another woman in my life. Very crazy. There had been a man in Monique's life. Not that she talked about him much. His name was Bruno. That was his real name. As Monique is hers. They met here in Paris.

Monique would drive out Fridays from Lawrence and stay through Sundays from teaching grade school. In summers she'd live with us weeks at a time. Monique was tall and trim. Hair cut just above her ears. A pail of fresh milk, as Buck called her. And blond nearly to cream. We lived together that way for about five years until she returned to Paris.

Well, we had Amos, a black lab of mine, and later, Murphy, a mutt that Monique found at a rest stop. Everywhere were chickens scratching and hens running to hide their eggs—plus rabbits and squirrels and cats mixed in for good measure.

At the beginning there was Milky, who was past her prime, but now and then I'd give her a try. I thought it might please the old cow to be of use, the ranch cats gathered under her, milling and meowing.

"You get in some good thinking putting your head into the side of a cow," Buck said when he saw me going into the barn with a bucket.

The first summer Monique stayed with me, she put her head into the side of Milky as much for what I'd told her Buck had said as for the cats.

"It works," she said.

"Good thinking?"

"Yes," she said.

"What do you think about?"

"Us. That you are *mon coeur*. 'A dear heart,' in English. I will teach you more French as you want to learn."

I went to get a Polaroid Ellen had bought when they first moved to the ranch.

Later that summer, Milky died one night and it was Monique who found her in the morning. Buck hooked up the backhoe to the tractor and dug a burial pit south of the Home-House, where, after Buck hired Patsy to clean and cook for us a year or so later, she planted her first garden, never knowing why it came on so well from the beginning—and for all the years afterward. It seemed a pleasure to keep the secret.

The evening we buried Milky, Monique sang a version of "The Night They Drove Old Dixie Down" in her fine alto voice, with the chorus as "The Night Old Milky Died," and there was no irony in her version, only woe, even though she had not known Milky but that summer.

"She's a fine woman," Buck said to me the next morning when we were alone over coffee. "A pail of fresh milk to be sure, but more than that."

Later, there was Moshe, a one-eyed tomcat that Patsy brought out to catch mice but whose specialty was not mice, but anything bigger than himself: chickens, box turtles—in addition to the pheasants, ducks, turkeys, rabbits and deer we'd hang in the well house behind my cabin. Moshe would get to the game with a leap and a hiss and hang on. I'd find him chewing as best he could on a shot mallard until he fell off and went to look for a yard rabbit. Without Milky and with the arrival of Moshe, the other cats hit the dusty trail. Buck used to say that the farms and ranches in Western Kansas were so far apart each had its own tomcat. Moshe was ours.

)(

One blue blizzard night the first winter after we hired Patsy she brought Moshe into the house and fed him grocery-store cat food.

"You know what that is?" Buck said, pointing at Moshe.

"A cat," said Patsy.

"That's the only animal in the world that can turn money into cat shit." It was Monique who gave Moshe his name.

Sometimes you'd see rattlesnakes. Two owls: Dame and Monsieur, "*Pas Blanche*," as Monique named them, saying that meant "Not White" in French. Doves came in and out of the shelterbelt. The summer he got rattlesnake bit, Moshe took himself into the heat of the south pasture to die.

"Leave him be," said Patsy when Monique thought she might drive him to the vet. "Leave him to himself. He knows what he's doing. When he's gone the fire ants will finish him. 'What goes around comes around'—Jesus-God."

We had hired Patsy to help with the chores around the Home-House, cook our meals, and make a garden—and for her company—in exchange for her wage and meals.

We were good company, and not hard to please with what she fixed: Stews and soups in winter at noon, what is called "dinner" in that country. Chicken or pig for supper in the evening. Buffalo meat from a bull Patsy's hippie nephew and his girlfriend won in a lottery and had us kill. Channel catfish out of the pond. Ducks we shot. Pheasants. A deer in winter. Cold beet and vegetable soups from Patsy's garden in summer. Salads as well from the garden for what Patsy called our "cesspool systems."

Patsy was no rose. Not even a shriveled flower at the stem's end. Mostly thorns—especially if you crossed her. And given to "Jesus-God." That was her word: Jesus-God. Also, we didn't live in Buckeye Township, Ellis County; we lived in *West Jesus Land, Kansas*. Every place else was *The Rest of America*.

If Patsy had a dress we never saw it. (Well, I did: once.) Summer or winter she'd wear blue-striped bib overalls and work boots. In winter she layered shirts and sweaters. In spring and early fall she'd wear T-shirts, and in summer, when it got up past "Hell's high roast number" (100), she'd wear nothing but her bib outfit and sockless boots.

"She might be naked under those overalls," I said to Buck one day.

"Some things are best not to imagine."

In the side straps and pockets Patsy carried pliers, gloves, a beer opener (bottle or can), bailing twine, a snub-nosed .22 revolver, golf balls she'd put in the hen's nests to fool them into setting, a small cloth bag for eggs, and, always hanging at her side, a hatchet for beheading chickens and snapping turtles on the cottonwood stump by her garden. Breakfast, dinner or supper, she'd take her meals with all her "armament attached." Patsy was built like her overalls, tools included.

Buck's ranch was small, but good grass. No plow land. Springs that flowed into the draws, deep water wells, one big pond and a few smaller ponds in the horse back pastures. We had windmills that fed the stock tanks, and there were limestone outbuildings from an abandoned homestead on the northwest quarter. Good fences, solid gates with deep-buried dead men to hold both corner posts straight. Stout corrals. Rattlesnake quarters with rock outcroppings and soapweed down to the river.

⋇

I shall always look on Paris with a loving eye. From my youth my heart has been hers. And the more I see of other lovely cities, the more I love her for herself.

—Montaigne

Thus, my first translation. If this finds you even if I do not, please know that in this way we are together again.

⋇

One day a few weeks after Patsy started working for us, Buck and I were in the kitchen drinking coffee and chewing the fat over bankers and women. Buck had a theory that it was better not to think about women or bankers by your lonesome because it would lead to "confusion and certitude." Better to talk about them with someone there to say "good thinking" or "bad thinking." Those were two of his favorite sayings. Not that the world was black and white to him, but some of it was.

"Talk is ventilation for the brain," Buck said. "Just like you need to open the vents and damper on the Woodsman now and then to keep it from smoldering and getting creosote in the flue pipe. You don't want smoke in your head."

"What else is there but 'certitude and confusion'?" I asked. "It seems to me if you have one, you don't have the other."

"They're opposite sides of the same half-dollar," said Buck. "Especially, when it comes to women and bankers. You get confused and then to clear your head, you think you need to get certain. But that's bad thinking. Nothing is certain." Because he was not given to clichés, he stopped there. About then we heard Patsy drive up. She'd check for eggs before she came in.

"We were just talking about women," Buck said when Patsy opened the door. He liked to get her started.

"If I spent as much time talking about men as you do women," she said, "you'd be eating the oilcloth off this table instead of breakfast. And bindweed instead of carrots—which at least would do your cesspool some good."

"Just about as much time as you talk to Jesus-God," I said. I liked to keep her going.

"Jesus-God is worth it," Patsy said. "I talk to Him when I'm doing dishes. You don't mind doing dishes or cleaning house if you and Jesus-God are talking. You guys come to Jesus-God or you'll get barbequed in Hell," she said, putting away her eggs.

"Well, at least that would be the end of it," said Buck.

"Not so," said Patsy. "You're never dead in Hell. The Devil barbeques your body parts for different evils. Curse Jesus-God and your tongue gets cut off and barbequed. Every body part that has offended Him gets barbequed."

"What about...?" I asked.

"That too," she said, "if you've had a propensity to whore-fuck. What's left gets tossed to the three-headed wolves to scarf down. *Demonically 13:23*." Like Thomas Jefferson, Patsy had her own version of the Bible.

"I see," I said.

"Black snake ate my golf ball," Patsy said as she poured herself coffee and joined us at the table. "But I got it back. Chopped his head off. I'll curl him down around one of my tomato plants for fertilizer. Waste not, want nothing." Then she fetched the Polaroid to snap our picture. Once Patsy found the camera she got big on taking pictures.

"Better to start a worm farm than stuff a coffin," Buck said. "Or toss us in the pond to feed the turtles."

"Not me," said Patsy. "I'm flying to Jesus-God when The Rapture comes." While Patsy finished her coffee, we ventilated our brains on Jesus-God, bankers, The Rapture, and whether turtle food or worm farms were a better way to go. Then Buck and I headed out to check cattle.

Paris

Tristesse (sadness). I have an editor in America who has written me in today's mail to ask for an essay on *sadness*. What prompted her request I know: in recent years her magazine has published a number of my stories, including the one with the character who now lives with me. She also hopes to come to Paris later this year. Hers is a quest for me; mine is a search for another.

My French is scattered in spite of Monique's efforts to teach me (she did in fact teach me *tristesse*), and it seems to me that *tristesse* is a better word for what it is than "sadness."

Maybe there is too much sentimentality in "sadness." And yes, I do see both here in Paris, especially if you count the homeless with their dogs, kept, I am told, because with animals of any kind the homeless cannot be arrested.

I do not know if my editor means sadness in that way—or in a person. Am I afflicted with *tristesse*, given my search? Is there more than a degree of difference? I am not sure my editor understands such distinctions. I am not sure she understands me.

There is a man on Rue Bonaparte who is especially curious because he is not so much woebegone as a man of more than modest accomplishment in another life: a man who went out one afternoon from a wife and family in a remote French village in the Dordogne to get a bottle of wine and never returned.

Here in Paris he has used what funds he has to buy a sturdy three-wheel bike with a tow-behind small camper of sorts. He arranges himself out of the way under an arch, and unlike the other homeless he does not beg, but instead has a small bowl set out should you want to leave some change. And a bowl for the dog as well—a dog that reminds me of Murphy. I am trying to make friends with "Murphy" by bringing him table scraps. As to the man, we do not talk but nod to one another. In his leaving where he came from to live in Paris we are *camarades*. And if my editor comes here she will observe that the man and I look alike. I think so myself.

I have also seen a woman now and then in a café on the Right Bank where I sometimes take a coffee. She has a battered mink coat she wears when the weather is cold and carries when it is not. I am reminded of a character out of a Jean Rhys novel: *Good Morning, Midnight*, I think. At first we just looked at one another, more recently we have begun to nod. I think we have resolved never to talk, but how I sense this (in myself and as well for her) I do not know. The transmigration of *tristesse*. And then there is this from Montaigne:

> *The Italians do well to use the same word for sadness, "la tristezza," as for malignity: for it is a passion as harmful as it is cowardly and base—and always useless.*

X

Our herd was about two hundred. First-calf heifers. They had been bought cheaper that way, even though we'd have trouble calving them—which we planned to do in January so we could beat the late summer market at the sale barn when everybody was bringing in their cattle before the grass dried up and winter came on. Supply and demand. But with the cattle market, it's mostly luck.

One day we lost two heifers on the Saline when they got into quicksand. I found them up to their bellies, dead, the water going around them, making eddies. Maybe one wasn't dead, but trying to rescue her was foolish. My horse got his front hooves stuck at the edge of the river, and I had to rear him up and spin around to firm ground. Across the river was Mencken Cody's ranch so when I got back I told Buck he might give Mencken a call about the quicksand should he have any cattle along the Saline. It was Mencken's Gomer bull we were using to mark the herd.

A week later when Buck and I rode back to check our fences the heifers were mostly skin and bones. Both heads were on the carcasses. Eyes gone.

"At least someone got to eat," Buck said. "'What goes around and comes around' isn't bad thinking." We rode back to the Home-House, and when we got there Patsy was ringing the yard bell for dinner.

There were lodgepole pine fences around both the Home-House and my cabin, and the larger yard of about five acres was fenced with barbed wire. In that yard were tool sheds, calving pens, horse stalls, and a storage garage where we worked on trucks and parked equipment. To the north, west and south ran a WPA shelterbelt of shrubs and trees, leaving the east side open. One year we found a beehive in a dead cottonwood tree on the south side. We let it get started until the following year, then every year after that I'd put on a long-sleeved shirt and gloves and stretch a ski-mask stocking cap over my head and dig out a few combs with a small trowel, while leaving most of it intact. From the honey Patsy made syrup and oatcakes.

We also had a pack rat named Gone. Whatever was missing: gloves, hats, light tools, a washed dish towel that blew off the clothesline, T-shirts left out overnight from a summer day, rags from the shop bench, once the ski mask I put on the porch of the cabin—it was Gone. For some unspoken reason we all agreed to leave Gone alone—with Buck only saying that what goes around doesn't always come back around.

"He is our archeologist," I said.

"What's that?" asked Buck.

"They find out who we were by sorting through our trash."

"Sort of like they are the socialists of the dead?" he asked.

"That will be Gone when he's gone," I said.

One Friday in late summer Monique was to come out after a teacher's workshop to stay a week or so until school started. Saturday was Patsy's birthday and the plan was to fix her a meal in the Whorehouse Room. That was the big room in the Home-House with a Woodsman stove at one end and a large fireplace at the other that we'd stoke up with cottonwood on special occasions. After Patsy started cooking and cleaning for us we let her decorate it.

"She wants to buy red wallpaper," I had said to Buck. "It's furry with gold gilt in it. And paint the window trim red." There were two windows on the north side of the room, on either side of the Woodsman. By this time Patsy and Monique had met and, for reasons that were mysterious to both Buck and me, become *chères amies*—as Monique put it.

"And hang framed mirrors," I said.

"Just as long as she doesn't get scared away for seeing herself," Buck said.

"And chandeliers. When she's done it will look like a whorehouse."

"Good thinking."

One weekend early in the summer when Monique came out we went to Hays with Patsy to buy what she wanted. She had us put down a purple shag carpet. She covered the chairs with deerskins, and the couch with a large bedspread that had a stag's head in the middle. We weren't allowed in with our work boots. I bought a player piano from the Woodcutter's Widow in Bly who was selling out piece by piece. The deal came with fifty rolls of old-time songs—all of them in good shape. Even though Monique could play the piano (and a guitar that she'd leave so she didn't have to bring it out each time), she'd pump the pedals and we'd all sing along: *You are my sunshine, my only sunshine, you make me happy when skies are grey, you'll never know dear, how much I love you, please don't take that sunshine away.* Patsy would join in.

"She can't carry a tune in a pickup," Buck said. But when we went "goodbye" with a stout glass of Black Jack, we didn't much care.

After I bought the piano, Buck and Patsy bought Monique a French horn we also kept in the Whorehouse Room.

"I don't know how to play it," Monique said when they gave it to her.

"Well, it's French and on sale," said Patsy, "and I know how you like France so..."

"I can learn. And thank you," Monique said. "Both of you." I suspect she knew it was Patsy's idea and Buck's money.

The next time out, Monique brought an enlarged photograph of the Dodge City Cowboy Band from the 1900s that she got from the Kansas Historical Society. It showed twenty or so bug-eyed and half-drunk cowboys with their instruments, some men lounging on the floor in the front, others on risers leading up to a lone woman, young to be sure, but not a pail of fresh milk, sitting on a set of very large longhorns. There were tubas and trumpets and tambourines. Drums and clarinets. One man was holding a pistol. But no French horns.

"For the Whorehouse Room," Monique said when she gave the picture to Patsy. It was framed in barn wood.

"I like the men with the tubas," said Patsy.

"They are upright E-flat altos," said Buck. "Not tubas."

"How did you know that?" Monique said.

"I used to play one in the high school band," Buck said.

"Then you can play my French horn."

"I only play upright E-flat altos," Buck said.

"I'd like 'The Red River Valley,'" said Patsy, when she saw that Monique had brought a book of French horn instructions and sheet music. For my part, I had bought a music stand also from the Widow Bly.

"I'll try," said Monique. "I'll try."

Over time we'd hear Monique doing what she could with the French horn, and when she was not around, we'd find Patsy giving it a polish.

"Jesus-God told me to keep it shiny for Monique," she said.

To Patsy's credit the Whorehouse Room was always clean, and it looked as if a high-dollar Dodge City dove of low moral character might leave her perch on longhorns and join us at the player piano to sing "The Red River Valley." And, as it turned out, the Whorehouse Room was where we had our Black Jack every night after work—but not before we had showered, tended to cuts and bruises, combed our hair (Patsy was big on combed hair) and put on clean clothes. "'Be clean and combed for Jesus-God once a day.' *Evaticus 7:3.*"

"Goodbye," Buck would say by way of a toast when he tipped his whiskey glass. *Goodbye,* so said we all as the pain of work began to fade. Patsy drank long-necked Coors.

After our Black Jack we'd usually go into the kitchen for supper. On Saturdays and Sundays we stayed in the Whorehouse Room, and Patsy (and Monique, if she was there) would bring the food to the big wooden trestle table that dead-ended on the west side just below where we'd hung the picture of the Dodge City Cowboy Band. The table had a long rough scar down the middle. Buck said the scar was a mystery, but he wouldn't say much more, and so we'd take turns telling stories of how the table got its flesh wound and why.

Sometimes Buck would tell a version, and if it was the real story or not, he never said. It was a routine we liked. No matter how we sat at the table, it was understood no one sat at the far end, now under the picture of the Cowboy Band, and how we understood that was our custom was not talked about.

When hunting season began, the Ranch Doctor would drive out from Lawrence. In exchange for taking him hunting, he'd give us physicals, and his last time out, he became part of Monique's *Whorehouse Room Colloquy.* As did we all.

Sometimes I'd cook for Patsy. She'd sit in the sunshine on the south side of the house by her garden, pulling on her long-necked Coors. She liked being called to dinner or supper instead of ringing the bell for the calling. Not always, but for a break. Small luxuries are better than big ones if you live in the country. And I liked fixing the meal. Even setting the table and washing up.

Buck didn't cook. Only slabs of venison on the pit grill when we shot a deer. Patsy knew how to make jerky, and we had a hand-crank meat grinder for everything but the good cuts. A deer could feed us through to spring if we portioned it out: steaks, ground meat for chili, a couple of roasts, jerky for the truck when we were windshield ranching. Patsy would mix the ground deer with the ground buffalo and call it "two-beast burger," and she'd use it for meatloaf, chili, or "two-beast burgers." We tanned and tacked hides on the south side of my cabin to cure.

Patsy grew hot peppers that she'd string and hang in the kitchen to dry for the chili. And braid onions and hang those in the well house. Keep carrots and potatoes covered with straw so sometimes we'd have them into December. She planted sweet corn and tomatoes and green and red salad peppers. One year she had me bring sand up from the Saline and mix it in on the south edge of the garden where she grew watermelon. She also asked for the ashes from the woodstove and the fireplace and she'd mix those into the topsoil. The garden got better until it became "abundant." It was a word Buck had once used and Patsy borrowed. "The abundance of Jesus-God," Patsy would say when looking over the garden. Most anything good in those days was "abundant" to her. Patsy liked words. We all liked words. *Propensity* was a favorite. "She's an *abundance* of Jesus, that's for sure," Buck would say after Patsy had gone off on one of her religious benders. "With a *propensity* for Hell," I said.

"That too," said Buck.

"Have you decided to tell her about Milky?" I asked.

"No. Let her have Jesus-God as the tomato deity and we'll worship the old cow." Patsy had me build a "moat" around her garden by putting up a chicken-wire fence so she could keep a dozen or so hens there to eat the grasshoppers before they got to her plants. The other chickens ran in the yard, but Patsy thought the best ones for cooking came from the moat because of the grasshoppers they ate. The yard chickens were for soup or stir-fries. And eggs.

"When Jesus-God made a chicken, He was thinking of women," Patsy used to say. "You take a chicken and a woman who knows how to pick it and she can feed all of West Jesus Land, Kansas, and half of The Rest of America, and be pleased to do so."

One spring when we had good rains the plum thickets around the edge of the ranch bloomed. I cut the flowers for Monique when she came out, and for Patsy as well.

"We'll have sand hill plums in the fall," Pasty said. "I can make jam of them."

"You can also put them on the table for treats," said Buck. Sometimes that fall when we were windshield ranching, Buck would get out and pick plums for ourselves and to take back to Patsy.

Paris

My diary seems to have grown a self unto itself; now there are three of us here in Paris, plus of course shades from the past as we go along, one of us (*moi*) looking over my shoulder at the other two—or maybe we are arm in arm.

In any case all of us wonder at my extensive details about the food in Kansas, given that here in Paris all along the *rues* and mansard roofs there are gifted cafés and restaurants.

My list of Kansas foods might be only a slim pamphlet, but Brillat-Savarin's *The Physiology of Taste* at over four hundred pages is a *très* fat one. I like his English title: *The Joys of the Table*. I hereby steal it for our Kansas fare.

It is my diary (he/she needs a nom de plume) who wonders why we were all more pleased with sand hill plums and caught channel catfish than a *homard thermidor*. And it is also true that all the time I lived there we never went out for dinner.

✕

We had horses to work the pastures down along the river; two old four-wheel-drive pickups with granny gears; a John Deere 4010 for ground we leased west of us to grow oats for the horses; a square baler (that was always breaking down) for the prairie hay when we could get a cutting, and for a small alfalfa patch in a creek bottom leading to the Saline. All of it mortgaged to the bank. Not the horses. Not the Home-House nor my cabin. Not Milky. They can't take what you ride or where you live. Or what's dead. It was good while it lasted, and to be fair to the fates, it lasted quite a while. Even with Ellen's death partway into it. And even after we were broke. There's a lot you can do without much money if you put your mind to it, and it's not a bad use of your mind. In this way, we ate well and lived well, being careful. For a long time nobody got badly hurt or sick. We stayed together.

When the end came, it was Patsy who helped me bury the dogs, dead two months apart, in the shelterbelt west of my cabin, their nametags nailed to a tree near their graves. With the Polaroid I took Patsy's picture by the tree, then we went to town where Patsy put on her dress for the service, what there was of it, just the two of us standing by the flat stone marker with no name on it. "I wonder where he went," said Patsy.

"Maybe nowhere in particular. Maybe somewhere," I said.

"Not to be found," Pasty said. "He once told me that was where he wanted to go."

After that we drove back to the ranch and Patsy packed up pots and pans, stuff, the French horn, books, and three live chickens to take to town. I helped her move. There was snow in the air. Later, Mencken Cody wrote me here in Paris to say Patsy had come back out to the ranch the following summer and they found her half-crazed in the heat and the wind of a bad August, tearing down the chicken moat around her garden and shooting pistol shots into the sky at the Anti-Christ. Mencken took her to Blaze to live with her sister.

〤

Since I have been in Paris I have written a dozen short stories, some of them set here, some in Western Kansas, others set one place or another in The Rest of America. I have published them in various magazines (including in my *triste* editor's magazine), and now I am arranging them for a book. The publisher is not a large New York firm, but rather a fine small publisher, and I am grateful for their offer. My name is Leo Murdock, but I use another name for my stories, and now for this book.

What I like about living in Paris is the distance it gives me on America, and paradoxically on Paris itself. I doubt a French writer would feel the same way were he or she to live in New York, and I cannot say why I feel a distance from Paris even as I am living in it. Perhaps if I were fluent in the language that distance would close. Translations of Montaigne help. Also, this from Twain (by my memory): "The French are amazing, even the children speak French."

The proof for the book of short stories came the other day. The cover is the picture of the Dodge City Cowboy Band—unless I save it for something else. I am to choose the title from one of the stories.

I need to think about it. And a dedication. Maybe a preface.

It has become a late fall or early winter here in Paris. Proust's memory is triggered by scents. Mine, as it turns out, by memory. The other day I found a bistro that served *poule au pot*, the flavor of it floating into Place Dauphine. I have not found *soupe éternelle*. I suppose I could make it myself but I don't cook here. Instead, I take a coffee and a *pain au chocolat* at the café where I first met the sad woman in the mink coat. Some days she is there, some days not. The same for me.

It is as we are avoiding each other in order not to meet one another: a woman out of a Jean Rhys novel probably does not want to step into the fiction of Western Jesus Land, Kansas—or even The Rest of America. Nor do I want to be absorbed into Rhys's *triste* world of misery and woe, even if she does write better than I do. Here's not looking for you, kid.

※

The Friday before Patsy's birthday, Monique got to the ranch at sunset just as Buck rode up on his horse, Canyon Snip, from checking cattle. Patsy had gone to town so we were on our own for supper, but I knew Monique would have something. And a meal for the next day—not that Patsy knew we had learned it was her birthday.

"What's the moon?" said Buck, still sitting in the saddle and looking east.

"The Harvest Moon," said Monique.

"Very good," said Buck.

"You want to ride?" said Buck, taking his foot out of the left stirrup. "Double. It will be like riding bareback."

"With a man in the moonlight not my lover?" She said. "Sure. And I've never ridden bareback."

"I'm not harmless," Buck said. "But I'm not dangerous, either."

"Supper is in the truck," Monique said, as she swung in behind Buck and off they went into the east pasture while I took a box of food and wine into the Home-House.

Monique had brought one of her homemade pizzas and several bottles of Chianti. I had made a salad from Patsy's garden. There was apple pie. And two rounds of cheese, both Italian.

As I was getting supper ready, I looked outside and saw them coming up to the yard; Monique swung off, patted Canyon Snip on the nose, opened the gate, then headed for the house while Buck went to the tack room.

"How was it?" I said. "Double with a tall handsome cowboy and bareback to boot."

"I'm going to recommend bareback to my daughters," she said.

That night while we ate we talked about horses and moons and wine and food: ventilation for the brain.

The next day we put Monique to work fencing. We had taken old wire off a mile or so of posts and were putting up new wire. You can pull it tight with fencing pliers if you're not running the wire along more than half a dozen posts. Doing it that way, you hear the creak of the wire, and the sound of the hammer when you tap in a new staple.

But this morning our run was long and Monique had driven the truck ahead of us so we wouldn't have to walk back to get it. Then before we got to her, she'd drive farther down. It doesn't sound like much for work, but it made the job quicker and that pleased her.

"Leo, you going to marry Monique?" Buck asked as we made our way up the fencerow toward the truck. I could see her sitting on the tailgate. She was watching us. When she saw us looking her way she waved.

"I haven't asked her," I said.

"She'll ask you," he said.

When we finished we went back to the Home-House where Monique began preparing Patsy's dinner, while I set the table in the Whorehouse Room. For a present Monique had brought an autographed book of paintings by Robert Sudlow, the Kansas painter of the prairie. We had signed it earlier that day, each of us adding "*un peu d'affection*," as Monique had asked us to do.

"I know him," Monique said, "and I had it autographed: *To Patsy of West Jesus Land, Kansas. Robert Sudlow.*"

The book was wrapped and put at the head of the table where Buck usually sat, but where Patsy would sit for this evening. Supper was a French meal: *poule au pot.*

"It means chicken in a pot," Monique said. "Henry the Fourth thought all his subjects should have *poule au pot* every Sunday."

I was in the kitchen with her slicing and dicing as she began putting the meal together, using some ingredients we had, but others she had brought: garlic, celery, parsley, bay leaves, juniper berries, leeks, small turnips, new potatoes—but not carrots, which were still coming on in Patsy's garden.

Earlier in the week I had killed and plucked a chicken and

kept it in my refrigerator. Also in my cabin Monique had put two bottles of Bordeaux and a Roquefort cheese.

"Instead of a birthday cake," Monique said to me, "I am going to make a chocolate soufflé. Since Patsy is not here, it is up to you, *tu*," she said, blowing me a kiss, "to find a dozen eggs."

"Me?"

"*Ah oui*," she said. "You are *vous* in French. Egg is *oeuf*. And bring the wine: *vin*. And *tu* is for 'you' between lovers. Got it? Later I will teach you that some nouns are feminine and others masculine. In the meantime you should use French words in whatever you write. You are an *auteur* in French."

"*Poule, tu, oeuf, vin, moi*," I said. "*Auteur, c'est moi. Oui?*"

"*Ah oui.* Now add: *un peu d'affection*," she said. "It means 'a little bit of affection.'"

"Plus *Pas Blanche*."

"*Bien*," she said. And winked. "Good."

I met Buck coming to the house and roped him into helping me look for the eggs; it took a while, but we got a dozen together, and while Buck brought them into the house I got the wine. Then we stayed in the kitchen to help as we could. Buck thought to have everything ready to surprise Patsy.

"If you had told her," Monique said, "she would have gotten dressed up. Women don't like being surprised as much as men do. They like better getting ready."

"How about we tell her next time around?" I said. "A year to look forward to it."

"That's a long time getting ready," Buck said. "And the future is not always that far off."

"She'd be pleased," Monique said.

Just then Patsy drove up and Monique handed Buck the wine and I took in the food. Monique got the French horn and when Patsy walked in she played a rough version of "Happy Birthday."

Patsy was bewildered, and for a moment joined in the song, singing as badly as ever until it dawned on her maybe it was her birthday she was singing about.

"I didn't bring a present," she said.

"We took care of that," Monique said. And here Buck got the book and handed it to her. Standing, she unwrapped it, looked at the cover with its celebrated *For the Villages, a Kansas Landscape* painting, and turned it over and over, then opened it to see our tributes and Sudlow's dedication—all of which she read aloud, thinking, to my ear, that she liked Monique's comment the best: *To the greater woman of the ranch, from the lesser one.*

"I'll put it with my Bible. For later," she said.

Then she looked at dinner all set out and the candles lit around the room and shook her head, saying nothing as she took the tools from her bib overalls: pliers, pistol, gloves, beer can opener, baling twine, golf balls, the hatchet, and, putting them with the silverware at her place, sat down smiling.

"Hello," said Buck, raising his wine glass by way of a toast. Hello, so said we all—even Patsy.

As we ate, each of us told a Scar Table story, mine being that Buck had caught a thief trying to steal his World War II souvenir Samurai sword and, using his Winchester model 70 .30-06 deer rifle (he had been out hunting, which I did not include because our Scar Table stories never had much exposition to them), fired off a round from his hip, the bullet passing along the top of the table leaving the scar. Where it went from there (into the body of the thief or into the wall now covered with Patsy's wallpaper) I did not tell, nor what happened to the thief, it also being our custom not to advance the plot from one of our stories to the next. Nor even to continue the story we had started. Nor weave it into the stories of the other authors telling theirs.

As for Patsy, she said it was not a bullet but a bolt of lightning from the end of Jesus-God's finger (Monique had once brought out an art book with Michelangelo's Sistine Chapel in it) that was a warning to "get right with the Lord" or get zapped with grave diggers going horizontal like Jesus-God would when he flew east to west not long from now. In the end we'd have arrows of lightning all over our bodies just like the heathens did to Jesus. "Fadictis 26."

When it came Buck's turn, he said he did not have a Japanese Samurai sword and never did have one, but now that he had shot a thief trying to steal it, he'd see what he could do about getting one from the Widow Bly, given that her husband had traded for many things over the years and she was now selling out.

Either that or he only wounded the thief, who fled through the kitchen with the sword that Buck never had in the first place, and probably was dead in a back pasture by now and we'd find him skin and bones like the quicksand-trapped heifers—but still holding the Samurai sword that we'd bring back to go with the story.

Beyond this, Buck said nothing, and none of us asked if he'd like to tell a story of his own, which apparently he did not. However, I remembered two he had already told about how the scar came to be. But both of those were before Patsy and Monique—as were two I had told. And we did not retell them, that also being our custom.

When it was Monique's turn, she said it was not Jesus who had been shot with arrows but Saint Sebastian, as depicted in a number of paintings from the Renaissance. As for the scar, she said a woman made it with her wrath.

"What about her wrath?" asked Buck.

"Well," said Monique, "the woman got pissed and scanned her eye down the table and the fierceness of her glare was white hot, and it burned the scar into the table from one end to the other, causing all the food and drinks that had been set out for dinner by her to boil and burn, and Lo! The men could neither drink nor eat until the Woman's wrath was calmed, now and forevermore:

Hermitica 6:22." Here she winked at Patsy, who said, yes, that was in fact Hermitica 6:22.

After Monique's story, we began to eat, although Buck suggested we would be wise to test our food should it burn our lips. Nobody asked why the Woman had become pissed, that too being left out of the narrative. Or how her wrath was calmed—if it was.

At the end of supper, Buck went over to the couch and from behind it got another present, not wrapped. It was a copy of Frederic Remington's painting *The Fall of the Cowboy*, and, like the Dodge City Cowboy Band photograph, it also was framed in barn wood.

"What's that?" asked Patsy, thinking, I supposed, she might be getting another present.

"It's my birthday as well," said Buck, "and I got this for myself."

"Is that true?" said Monique, to which there was no answer as Buck turned to Patsy and said: "For the room you use upstairs. I'll hang it tonight so you might as well stay after we clean up." Patsy agreed and stood to give Buck a Paris cheek kiss, asking Monique if she'd done it right, which she had.

It was later that night when Patsy came to my cabin to say Buck had walked out of the Home-House and had not returned, and what did I think we should do? I got dressed, as did Monique, and we walked into the yard. His truck was there. The horses were standing by the outer fence, all but Buck's, Canyon Snip.

"Has he gone for a ride?" Monique said.

"Yes."

"Where?"

"Maybe nowhere in particular. Maybe somewhere."

Then we saw him coming out of the night with the moon on his shoulders and Canyon Snip holding his head up against the bit as he always did, even if Buck was not pulling it into his mouth.

"He hasn't seen us," I said. "Let's go inside."

"Do you think it is his birthday?" Monique asked. I said I did not know.

)(

More snow in Paris today. *Neige* in French: feminine. There is also cold and wind on the radio and in *Le Monde*. Like others I will look up at the snow coming down as I walk to Chez Denise on the Right Bank near Les Halles for lunch because it has fine *lapin*. Rabbit: masculine. Also, as the restaurant is not far from where my Jean Rhys woman takes her coffee, I wonder if we will pass one another, and if so nod, and this will be the end of it.

Back now: no Jean Rhys woman. Among those folk: not found.

)(

The big pond in the north pasture was fenced off so cattle couldn't get into it. There was a pipe through the dam into the stock tanks below. Early on I built a raft of oil barrels and wide board planks and floated it to the middle, where I anchored it with an old engine block. Every once in a while I would pull the engine block up to let the raft drift with the breeze from one part of the pond to the other, then re-anchor it.

In summer, if we had worked the horses hard, Buck and I would take them to the pond for a swim. We'd unsaddle and ride into the water bareback and, slipping off to the side, get a swim for ourselves. I put this in a story of mine, turning Buck into the mad populist down the road whom he much admired. When she was out, Monique would ride and swim as well.

Springs fed the pond from draws to the west and east, and from the bottom. The ones from the bottom made for cold patches. When Monique would feel one, she'd do a surface dive down into it. Her legs would come up for a moment, and then slip away. She could hold her breath a long time—and she never came up where she went under; sometimes she'd resurface halfway across the pond. I'd be treading water looking for her.

"Here, over here." If no one was around she'd swim nude. We both would.

"How did Buck's wife die?" Monique asked me one day on the raft.

"A grain truck from the feedlot ran a stop sign on the Seven Hills Road and hit her broadside."

"Did she live long?"

"Too long."

Monique was quiet.

"Someday I'd like to have a picnic on the raft," she said.

"Sure," I said. I thought she might be buying time to say something else.

"Does it have a name?"

"The raft?"

"Yes. Did you name it?"

"We didn't think to do that," I said.

"Could we name it for her?"

"Ask Buck," I said.

Monique didn't ask Buck about naming the raft. But between us we named it for Ellen—but it was not "Ellen," as I have written before. The next time we had a picnic on the raft Monique christened it with a champagne toast: the *Ellen* (but as Monique knew her real name we used that).

Patsy and Monique liked to fish the pond for the largemouth bass and the big white-meat channel cat. Snappers that we'd put in a rain barrel by the garden and fatten with scraps, and milk to sweeten the taste. When they got big enough, Patsy would put a broom handle into the barrel and, after the snapper hit it, haul him to the chopping block to "cleave his parts apart."

"Most of what's a turtle is in his head," she'd say, as its body ran around the yard until it stopped, the head still snapping elsewhere. If Moshe was around he'd go for the body.

"Where'd you learn about turtles?" Monique asked.

"When he's done snapping," Patsy said, "toss him in the garden unless Moshe wants him," not answering Monique's question. Many of our conversations about it went this way.

"Where'd Patsy learn to clean snapping turtles?" Monique asked Buck.

"With some women, the cleaning of snapping turtles is genetic memory," Buck said. "What comes around, comes around." As with other pronouncements of Buck's, I could never be sure the manner of mirth intended. If any.

"It's like 'transmigration,'" I said.

"What's that?" Buck asked.

"'What comes around, comes around.' Sometimes in bits and pieces. Sometimes not."

"Good thinking."

You must not confuse your needs with your desires.
—Montaigne

Being here in Paris writing a diary with the title *For Not Finding You*, in an apartment with a view of the Pont des Arts, in a city where I walk a lot in hopes of finding you, I am not confused about my needs and desires: they are the same. I do not have the French for that: *tant pis.*

Patsy had an apartment in town, and although we knew where it was, we had never been inside. But we had been in the room she used at the Home-House. She would bring pictures she had painted and hang them on the walls. There was no perspective.

Her sense of color was poor. All of them were scenes at the ranch: Views of her garden. The yard. The Pastures. Portraits of Moshe, Murphy, and Amos. The horses.

There was one of a windmill that pumped water for the stock tanks looking south and west. She never seemed to have her paints, and we never saw her make sketches, so she must have done the paintings from memory—or from the Polaroid. Every now and then she would take some back to Hays and bring others out. When she'd leave, we'd go upstairs to see what was new.

Under her bed she kept a portrait of Buck that I suspected she'd hang when she stayed over and took down when she left. I knew about it because one day I hid a present for Monique there. I never told Buck.

"That's looking west," said Buck one day in the room. "How come the trail road doesn't go to the stock tank like it should? It's more up in the air than on the ground."

"She's not that kind of painter," Monique said. Monique wasn't a painter, but she had majored in art history and her talk with us was "salted"—that was Buck's word—with references to paintings. The pond was right out of Corot. Patsy could have been painted by Toulouse-Lautrec. Buck by John Curry. Monique told me her hope was to teach American art history in France. Her French was good enough, she thought. She wanted to teach the French about the American painters: Sloan, Hopper, Bingham. They knew about Mary Cassatt because she was one of theirs. Also Whistler.

"The French can be provincial," she had said. "And proud of it." Monique brought out her art books and showed us the paintings she was talking about, and when she did, she'd let Patsy keep the books until she returned. You could see Patsy looking at them on the Scar Table. She was very careful.

"I wash my hands before I touch the Bible or Monique's books," Patsy said. "And not in dishwater." Later, this was true for her Sudlow birthday book as well.

When we showed Monique Patsy's paintings, she said they were "vignettes" in the American primitive tradition. For me a vignette was a small story.

"It's paintings as well," Monique said. "See how there are no edges or frames on her landscapes, how they fade off the canvas as if there is a mystery beyond the edge? That makes them vignettes. Not that she knows, which is what makes her an American primitive. There have been many of them from the eighteenth century to today."

"Art is long, but life is short," said Buck. Later, Monique asked me where Buck might have gotten his aphorism, and I said I didn't know.

⚜

Feeling mortal today given what I know lies ahead in my diary, I find this in Monique's Montaigne: *If you don't know how to die, do not worry. When the time comes, Nature will give you instructions; she will even do the task for you.*

I have said so long to everybody but myself.

The latter is not true in my case.

⚜

In summers Monique would spend weeks at a time with us before going back to Lawrence for a few days to check her mail. I'd send her a postcard before she left so she'd have something besides bills. I wouldn't tell her and after a while she came to expect them, but it still pleased her. We lived this way, back and forth, until Monique left for Paris.

"I think I want to get married," Monique said. We were on the *Ellen*.

"Why?" I said.

"It's something I'd like to do," she said. "Do you want to get married?"

"I don't know," I said. She was quiet for a moment. The cotton-woods around the pond were just starting to drop their leaves. When they do that, they flip in the breeze, first one side out then the other. I could see Monique looking at them.

She got up and dove into the water. She was nude as we had been lovers. This time she swam on the surface, doing a head-out-of-the-water breaststroke. Once I saw her shudder.

"Hit a cold patch?" I said.

She did not answer. She swam in widening circles around the raft, and then when she got close to the bank, she stood up. She was one of those women who are beautiful even far away. It was only later that I felt the weight in my mind of what I had said. And not said.

She did a shallow dive into the water and swam the crawl back to the raft. We spent the rest of our time on the raft talking about other things.

After our swim, Monique and I went back to the Home-House. Patsy had arrived, and while she cooked, Monique set the table. Buck and I took the truck into the pastures to check the heifers, and then drove to Hays to get supplies for various repairs. When we got back I helped Buck unload the truck before I went to my cabin for a shower while he tended to the horses. Earlier than usual I heard the bell ring, and when I walked out it was not Patsy ringing it, but Monique.

"It's not time yet," she said. "I just wanted you out of the cabin so I could put on something nice for supper without you seeing it first."

She had a yellow dress she'd bought after she'd read a story of mine where the character says yellow is his favorite color. When she came back, that's what she was wearing, but neither of us said anything about how it was special. Nor about what had happened on the *Ellen*. In the meantime there was the bustle of Patsy, who ran us out onto the front porch so as not to be in the way. Buck was at the east edge of the yard.

"What's he doing?" said Monique.

"Talking to the horses."

He had cattle cubes in his pocket and was feeding them.

Duke was a chowhound; he'd whinny to be fed. I could see Buck scratch the white arrow on his forehead. He seemed a horse who understood affection. Rare in the breed. Angel had her ears back, which meant she was "pissed about being pleased," as Buck would say.

There was a slight rise east of where Buck stood, beyond which you could see the top of a windmill that ran a water well pump. Some of the other wells we had put on small gasoline engines to run water into the tanks for cattle. But this one we kept active, for what reason I did not at first understand.

That pasture was where we kept our horses, and they could get water either at the edge of the yard from a small stock tank or at the windmill. Now they were up close.

We had five: Angel, Canyon Snip, Charlene, Duke, and my horse, Chief Lightfoot. We'd take turns riding all of them except for Charlene, a mare that had been Ellen's. She had bred her using Mencken Cody's stallion, and the foal, Duke, came just before Ellen died. All had kind eyes but Angel. Chief and Canyon Snip could be stubborn, but not angry about it.

If you don't ride a horse now and then, they can become difficult. Patsy didn't ride: "Anything a woman wraps her legs around is going to give her trouble," is what she'd say when asked about it. Nothing more, even though, when Buck once asked if she'd ever been married, she only said that her sister Testy had been.

"He was as ugly as a bucket of assholes and smelled twice as bad."

Monique liked Angel best, but she was a small American saddle horse with an independent streak and Monique was not a confident rider. Sometimes I'd use Angel to check cattle, and in that way she'd get ridden in advance of Monique coming out. Once, when I got in the saddle, Angel reared, and I put my fist to the top of her head, which usually would bring her down. But this time she flipped onto her back. I pitched off to the left and hit the ground. I looked to the right and watched the saddle horn dig into the dirt. Buck had seen it all.

"An inch to the north with that saddle horn and I've got dead help," he said when he came over. "Dead help is bad thinking." Angel got up and was about to bolt, but Buck grabbed her reins. "Dead help doesn't come back around except as turtles for Patsy's rain barrel."

"At least I'll be snapping."

"My father was killed by a horse," Buck said as he walked Angel in figure eights. I got back in the saddle.

"I didn't know that," I said.

"Best let Monique ride Charlene," he said. "I'll take her out to settle her down. It's past time she gets ridden. Maybe even bred again. I'll ask Mencken."

Buck opened the gate to the north pastures and I headed out on Angel to check the cattle. Later that day and a few times that week, I'd see Buck on Charlene but said nothing. Thinking back over those years, what went unsaid seemed natural. Including what I promised Buck not to write here—not that he would know. Still.

That night we took the meal to the Scar Table, and instead of a story, Buck told Monique how I was almost killed by Angel, and that she could use Charlene if she liked. Later, back at my cabin, Monique asked why I hadn't told her what happened, and I said I didn't want to frighten her, but that it was also Buck's way of letting her ride Charlene.

"She was Ellen's horse," I said.

As we went to bed, I sensed Monique wanted to say something, but did not. Later in the night I got up and went outside to look at the moon, now high above us. My leaving did not wake Monique. Or maybe it did. I should like to ask.

X

I have kept the Pont des Arts postcard you sent me from Paris all these years. First, as a bookmark, then later by itself on whatever desk of mine. Now the one here where I am typing.

In the cabin I had a small table where I wrote and over it I put a plate of glass under which I arranged snapshots: Me and Buck at the kitchen table. Patsy with a big watermelon. Monique on Charlene. Buck. Moshe with the good-sized rat. A headless snapping turtle. Chief Lightfoot. Monique and Milky. Monique. A basket of eggs. The French horn. Monique. Monique.

For a while I'd keep it script-side up (her handwriting a sad pail of fresh milk), then down, the picture of the Pont des Arts up. I took it with me when I left the ranch.

I have it here, Pont des Arts up. What does it mean that I cannot turn it over? *Tristesse*?

"Maybe her family will tell you where she is," Buck had said. But after that, he didn't say anything more—nor did I. Nor did they know.

)(

It stayed warm for all of September and into early October when we caught a small snow, and then it warmed into a long, soft Indian summer. The Ranch Doctor decided to come out to shoot doves and early ducks instead of waiting for pheasant season, and that meant we'd move up the Colloquy to mid-September.

The Friday of the October snow the bank called again, but Buck just hung up, refusing them even the gift of profanity.

"It has snowed in Kansas every month except August," he said when we finished our coffee before we went out to check on the heifers. It was a soft, wet snow. It hadn't been that cold but the wind had been hard all night and into the early morning. There were drifts into the draws, but the ground was warm and you could see water running through the snow.

We spotted Mencken Cody's Gomer before we found the herd. He was still marking and that meant we'd have to bring the heifers up to the corals for insemination. You had a few days after you saw the blue patch. We could have inseminated them ourselves, but we weren't set up for it, so we called the vet when we had half a dozen or so ready.

Over the next rise and down into a big cutout below the dam to the pond was the herd. They had found a place out of the wind. And grass as well. It was their first snow, but they knew what to do. It was a sight. They were bunched up like they had not been all summer and into the fall, bawling and milling. I spotted three new ones for breeding. Buck saw a fourth.

A coyote hustled over the hill to the river. As they do, it stopped to look back. Sometimes there were deer along a line of cotton-woods to the west and north of where the herd was, but not this morning. Wild turkeys, though. I could have taken one, but the shot would have spooked the heifers.

In the pickup were the cattle cubes. I climbed into the bed with a scoop shovel, and Buck drove along slowly while I laid down a line. We had fed the heifers cattle cubes a few times before so they'd know what they were—and to follow the truck if we needed to move them. Now we were just trying to pour energy to them. They'd need more in the evening.

"You want to horseback the marked ones up to the yard?" Buck asked as we drove to the Home-House.

"Sure."

"I'll drop you off to get saddled," he said. "There is something I want to do."

"Yes," I said. I knew where he was going.

Buck and I had scattered Ellen's ashes in places she especially liked: the line of cottonwoods where we had just found the heifers; among the old homestead of limestone buildings that was abandoned by the time Buck and Ellen bought the quarter; onto the waters of the pond, standing on the east side that day because of the wind; some at the top of the breaks that ran into the Saline. And one place Buck kept to himself, taking the last of her ashes with him.

That day we had driven the pickup far into the west pasture where there wasn't much but grass and a few rills. No trees. A small tank of a pond that was dry most years. Beyond the tank we'd use horses to work cattle. It had been warm during the days, but at night—and it was getting to be evening when Buck had me drop him off—it could get brisk quickly. There might be more wind in the air by sundown. Where he got out would be two miles from the Home-House.

"I can come back to get you," I said out the window.

"I'll walk," he said.

An hour later, just as the butane yard light started its slow glow, he came into the house. That night he made his Black Jack toast for the first time. We had chicken from a crockpot. This was before Patsy.

X

"What are we going to do about the bank?" I said when I came into the house after bringing up the heifers. Buck had passed me in the truck and was sitting in the kitchen. Outside, it was warming up. It wouldn't melt all the snow, but most of it.

"Let them figure out what they're going to do about us first," Buck said. "Sometimes it's best not to talk about troubles when they are on your back." What we didn't know was that the bank was trying not to go broke itself by taking us down.

"Monique coming out this weekend?" said Buck.

"That's the plan. Tonight after school, if they didn't get snow east of us, like the radio says."

"Does she know about Saturday?"

"I told her." Saturday was the date Ellen had died.

"There were some teal on the pond this morning," he said.

"I saw them."

"Do you think she'd eat teal?"

"I think she would. Would you rather have a turkey? They'll be back below the dam later today."

"Teal," Buck said. "How about that wine she brings?"

"What about it?"

"Maybe she'd bring something special for the teal."

"I'll call and ask. You want me to shoot the teal?"

"Let's both go," he said. "But we need to get the vet out for the heifers."

"Fine by me," I said.

After the vet came, we drove into Hays for errands. By the time we got back, there was no snow on the roads, only in the bar ditches, and that was melting fast. I found myself thinking that in an hour or two Monique would be on the highway, and four hours later she'd be at the ranch. It would be dark, but we'd wait supper for her. I'd left a message at the school about the wine.

"You want to take the teal now or tomorrow morning?" I said, as we were coming up the lane.

"Now," said Buck. "Let's feed the heifers while we're at it."

We shot the teal not long before Monique arrived. They came in at sundown. Buck shot two as they made a pass by our blind, and I shot two more when they came back a second time. We'd gutted them and hung them from the cross pole in the front yard with the dinner bell. I thought about Moshe and how he'd be trying to get to them with a leap to hang on.

Monique got to the ranch just after sunset. We had a good-sized moon to the east when she drove in. I had been standing in the yard looking for her lights. She drove a secondhand pickup with a spotlight through the roof, and when she'd make the turn off the highway onto the Buckeye Road, she'd flip on the spot-light. From two miles away you could see her coming. "A smoke signal," she called her light. Ten minutes later she'd be up the lane and in the yard. Driving in at night, she'd put the spotlight on me, then turn it on and off, so I'd be in the dark for a moment then in bright light.

"Sing!" she'd say, when she got out of the truck. "When the spotlight's on, you're supposed to sing."

Like Patsy, I can't sing; only in my case, I know it. Monique could sing. A lovely alto voice: Maria Muldaur lyrics. "We worked so hard, we died standing up." "Midnight at the oasis, put your camel to bed." "Hasn't it been a long…" Run a song through once, and she'd have the tune and the words. Even from the radio.

Buck liked the older songs: "The Way You Look Tonight," "A Small Hotel," "Dancing on the Ceiling." "The Last Time I Saw Paris" was a favorite, as it was with Monique. "April in Paris" as well. Buck had said he didn't want to go to Paris, he just wanted to imagine it. As he seemed pleased with himself for saying so, neither Monique nor I ever asked him what he imagined Paris might be like, but once he told me I could make it up for him. As I am doing: *Très en retard*. And for myself as well.

"The man at the liquor store didn't know what kind of wine went with teal," Monique said, "but he suggested Cold Duck."

"Sounds reasonable," said Buck, who had come out.

Buck knew nothing about wine, and I had learned what I knew years before when Monique and I had bought a mixed case of French wine (including a few bottles of the expensive Saint-Émilion) from money we earned collecting mistletoe out of the trees along the Wakarusa and selling it to the university faculty for Christmas. Back at her apartment she would tie the mistletoe with ribbons into bunches. I had an old Studebaker, and we'd drive around to the professors' houses. Monique would go up and make the sale. She was good at it. A dollar a bunch. Two dollars for three. We were told to age the Saint-Émilion for many years, something we failed to do.

"I brought us a better wine," Monique said and smiled. Then she gave Buck her Paris-Cheek-Kiss, brushing her cheek against

Buck's, first on one side then the other. Buck had to bend over for Monique, which he did with ease.

In those days we grew beards for winter, and Buck's was just coming out, as was mine. In the spring we'd choose the date to shave them off. One year, mine was in honor of A. B. Guthrie, whose novels I was just then reading. Another year it was on the birthday of the playwright William Inge, who was ahead of me at the university. When *Picnic* came to Hays, it was Patsy who said that all the men were watching Kim Novak during the dance scene while—and here Monique finished Patsy's sentence—"all the women were watching William Holden."

Buck picked the defeat of Custer the year I picked Inge. The next year he chose June 17, the date the Bonus Army's bill was defeated in Congress, and he stayed with those two, Custer on even-numbered years, the Bonus Army on odd-numbered ones.

"My dad was in that march to Hooverville," Buck had said. "He wasn't hurt, but he had a friend who was killed." As with many of his other observations, Buck did not expand, and you got the sense he didn't want to.

"Pretty soon you'll look like Curry's John Brown," said Monique to Buck as we walked toward the Home-House. "Just don't let bugs get in your beard, otherwise I'll have to shake hands when we meet."

"Everybody's got to have a place to live," Buck said, as he scratched his cheek.

"Good moon," said Monique, turning to look east at its climbing.

"Do you know this moon?" said Buck.

"I do not," said Monique.

"It's going to be the Hunter's Moon when it gets full," said Buck, and pointed at the teal hanging by my cabin with Moshe underneath.

"My heroes," said Monique, and gave Buck another Paris-Cheek-Kiss and me one as well. "What's a summer moon called?"

"Ellen called them 'Lamplighter Moons,'" said Buck. "By their brightness you could find what you'd lost in the yard." He paused and looked east, then: "One night we walked into this pasture to search for a bullwhip of mine that had come loose from Canyon Snip earlier that day. We could have waited until morning but..." Here he stopped and turned to walk back to the Home-House. I picked up Monique's bag and took it to my cabin as she went with Buck.

Patsy had made buffalo meatloaf for supper, the kind where you put whole hardboiled eggs in it, so that each piece might have a slice of egg in the middle, like a yellow eye. That's what we called it: "Yellow-eye buffalo meatloaf."

Patsy would also make One-Eyed Jacks: slices of bread with the middle cut out into which she'd crack an egg and fry it in the Griswold. Sometimes she'd put in a ring of link sausage and bring the frying pan to the table, where we served ourselves. Other times she cut a slice of cheese to put over the egg-eye. We'd get these for either breakfast or dinner. "Enough to feed Coxey's Army," Buck would say.

"Stay," Monique said to Patsy when she saw she was getting ready to leave for Hays.

"I brought you some French beer."

"I didn't know the French made beer," said Buck.

"Very good beer," said Monique. "Do stay."

"I think you two got better things to do than sit around with me after supper," she said, looking at me.

"Oh, he can wait," said Monique, and helped Patsy out of her coat. I could have taken it badly, but we were not like that with one another. And whatever had happened on the raft earlier that summer between us seemed to have faded.

We went into the Whorehouse Room, where Buck poured himself a Black Jack and said his traditional goodbye, even though it hadn't been all that bad a day. Monique opened a bottle of the wine she'd brought and a bottle of beer for Patsy.

"'La Belle Dame sans Merci,'" said Monique as she turned the beer bottle to Patsy so she could read the label. "It means 'the beautiful woman without mercy.'"

"Well, half that's me," said Patsy, and took a pull from the bottle even though Monique had put out a glass.

We drank and talked a bit: about the snow that had come through and how quickly it had melted. About Monique's drive out. French beer. Our beards and what date we had selected in the spring to shave and why. How soon the Ranch Doctor would come and Monique could have her Colloquy. That kind of talk until we went into the kitchen for the buffalo meatloaf and baked potatoes, after which Patsy cleaned up and Monique and I went to my cabin.

"The word for snow in French is *neige*," she said, looking at a small patch to the north of my cabin that had not melted. "It is feminine. And the word for rabbit," she said, as in the moonlight we could see one at the edge of the shelterbelt, "is *lapin*, which is masculine." Then we went inside.

⚹

Another letter in today's mail from my editor wanting to know how the essay on sadness is coming along and when she might visit me here in Paris. There is no essay on sadness (or *tristesse*) unless I cut one out of what I am writing and that seems a violation of what I am writing. As to my editor's visit, it seems an unfounded fascination on her part: indeed, she is about my age and attractive in many ways, and while we have met a number of times, we were not lovers; nor did it occur to me that either of us wanted to be that. I thought she was married, and now that I think of it, maybe she was and it has gone badly. The stuff of fiction but told from what point of view? Maybe I should write it and send it to her magazine—however, it is not in my character to do that. But by what means do I tell her not to come? I can find nothing in Montaigne to advise me.

✕

At times after dinner Buck might go back to the Whorehouse Room where he'd read. In the morning I'd find him there, not asleep in a chair with a book in his lap as you might expect, or on the couch near the woodstove, but sacked out on an old army cot he kept there, for what reason he never said.

"He doesn't want to get into their bed alone," Monique said when I told her about it. "It's probably a memory of her."

"From something he's been reading?" I said.

"Maybe," she said. "Was he with her when she died?"

"Yes." But I didn't say anything more—not what the doctors had said in the hospital.

Sometimes when we'd wake up in the morning, Monique and I would stay in my cabin past noon.

There was a small window at the head of our bed in the loft where we slept that I had put on hinges.

"I don't think we can get out," Monique would say each time she'd open it. What she was really saying was that she could probably squeeze through, but I was too big. In those days I had half a grain-sack belly from eating too much of Patsy's food.

"Let's try," I'd say. "You first."

And out she'd go and down the ladder and call to me from the ground. But I always found some excuse not to follow. We came to call it the *Thin Man Window*.

One day I made a pot of soup from a mason jar of Patsy's tomatoes, her onions, and chicken broth. Chicken as well. Frozen corn she'd put up from the garden. Peas. Bits of leftover rabbit and pheasant we shot and froze the year before.

Monique had brought soup of her own. She mixed our soups

together and we had it for lunch; then she put it on the woodstove with a trivet underneath.

"*Soupe éternelle*," she said. "It's what the French call it when you keep it going." She also had brought bread—a hard-crust dark bread that she'd make, and that Buck liked but Patsy did not—although she would use it for her One-Eyed Jacks.

"Not gooey enough," Patsy would say, and bring out a loaf of Wonder Bread. She was also fond of Velveeta cheese.

"I don't see how a woman who cooks so well and grows her own garden, and cleans fish and snapping turtles, can like Wonder Bread and Velveeta cheese," Monique said to me one day.

"And Spam."

"No!"

"Yes."

One day as we were heading over to Buck's for lunch, Monique said, "Do you remember the time Moshe came to the door with a large rat?" For once he'd caught something he could handle and seemed proud of it. It was the first time we'd talked about Moshe since he'd died; not even Patsy had said anything about him. I was about to say something about Milky and our first summer together, but did not. In these ways we had learned to say things that we had kept unsaid, and keep others not said.

"Does Patsy know about today being the day Ellen died?" said Monique.

"Yes."

✕

When I was a student my writing teacher told me to type out a passage from an author I admired. Her idea was not that I would then want to imitate the author, but that I would begin to learn how a writer's mind works: "Details and craft make art," I remember her saying. "Scholars and critics make the themes and meanings."

Over the years there have been many texts I copied in part:

Porter's "Rope"; Crane's "The Bride Comes to Yellow Sky"; Salinger's "Teddy"; Nabokov; Flannery O'Connor; the end of *Huck Finn*. But I started with the opening of Jack London's "To Build a Fire."

Now, here in Paris, having just walked back from a small café I know on Place Saint-Michel where Hemingway wrote "Up in Michigan," I type this from his *Moveable Feast*:

A girl came in the café and sat by herself at table near the window....I looked at her and she disturbed me and made me very excited. I wished I could put her in the story, or anywhere, but she had placed herself so she could watch the street and the entry and I knew she was waiting for someone....

...I've seen you, beauty, and you belong to me now, whoever you are waiting for and if I never see you again, I thought. You belong to me and all Paris belongs to me and I belong to this notebook and this pencil.

Then I went back to writing...and then I looked up and looked for the girl and she had gone. I hope she's gone with a good man, I thought. But I felt sad.

I know the feeling.

⋊

Sometimes Patsy would come out on Saturdays, but sometimes not. For sure she never came on Sundays. She'd go over to Blaze where her sister Testy held prayer meetings in the Pool Room Tavern. Often there were only the two of them; other times a few folk from around Blaze and Bly would show up, more for stories to tell than for religious instruction.

According to Patsy and Testy, when the End-Time comes Jesus-God is going to fly over Kansas east to west at thirty thousand feet, arms spread for wings. Legs apart like a wishbone. As He flies, the holy power of His body will suck up the Believers and leave the rest of us to roast. A Believer could choose the place on Jesus where they wanted to be attached.

"Like ticks," said Buck. "The best way to get them out is with the hot end of a burned match. That way you don't leave the head."

"Testy wants an earlobe," said Patsy. "She won't tell why. You guys are going to get burned black like you were cooked on that ground pit you use for deer steaks unless you get right with the Lord. Hell is going to bubble up from the innards of earth and catch it on fire, topsoil, cattle, pheasants, soapweed and all. Even that pond will be burning. Not just boiling. Burning. 'Water will turn to a lake of flame.' *Jerake* 4:36."

The week we had the prairie fires Patsy was sure she'd see Jesus coming across the sky and started for Blaze to be with Testy. Not to be together on an earlobe, though. Patsy was undecided between the scar on Jesus's right palm or the scar on His left foot. "You get straight with the Lord before the Devil roasts you like a hotdog on a stick," she said before she drove down the lane, the smoke getting thick to the north of us.

"Has she decided between the hand and the foot?" Buck said, as Patsy drove off.

"I didn't ask," I said.

It wasn't long before Patsy had to come back. They'd blocked off the road because of the smoke and the fire. She stood in the yard looking in the sky for Jesus.

"Could you see the fire on the ground?" Buck asked.

"Yes," Patsy said. "It was over by Mencken Cody's place. Coming our way."

"Was it jumping the roads?"

"The cow piles were," Patsy said.

"On fire?"

"Yes." All this time she was looking at the sky.

"That's the way it spreads," Buck said to me. "The cow flops catch fire and sail on ahead with the wind."

"Flying flaming Frisbees of shit," Patsy said. "It's the way the world is going to end. In a blizzard of flying flaming Frisbees of shit."

"Is that what it says in the Bible?" Buck said.

"Ravitics 3:26," said Patsy and walked into the house to fix dinner.

"How does she know about Frisbees?" I asked Buck.

"Her hippie nephew and his girlfriend," said Buck. "They throw the Frisbee back and forth across the Saline. Naked."

"I never saw that," I said.

"I wish I hadn't," Buck said.

We went inside where we got a sermon: It turns out that while the real Jesus is going east to west, a fake Jesus is going west to east, and if, as you are roasting away in pasture ponds of fire or getting pelted by flaming flying Frisbees of shit, you try to repent at the last moment, Jesus-God knows you're a fake and up you go to the west-to-east Jesus, where you get sucked into his bloodstream which is full of AIDS, and there you live all covered with blood and sores forever and ever and ever. Better to stay in Buckeye Township and get cooked.

"Her version of Job," Buck said.

)⟨(

There is somewhere a draft story of mine about a character (not the one with whom I am living) who gets a case of tinnitus. But I cannot find it on my Mac Pro, maybe because I misspelled it, or maybe because the draft was written on the ancient typewriter I once used in the cabin in West Jesus Land. No matter: his malady is now mine, and it has grown stronger in recent days. What was a faint and distant tingle has now become a small persistent ring, as if someone from somewhere were trying to get into the room of my memory. My character went to the American Hospital in Paris from which I have just returned. There, a doctor dressed in a white lab coat got out what looked to me like first one tuning fork and then another, each time hitting them with a metal swizzle stick until finally, four forks into the process, he said (in Franglais) that I had the "hearing of a *vieillard*." I suspected his meaning but I looked it up anyway: old, aged, masculine. *C'est moi.*

Shots were prescribed (in French) on a small piece of paper, and I was told I should go to a clinic on the Île de la Cité. However, I must note two things: I am not that old, and oddly, just going to the American Hospital to have myself evaluated has caused the ringing to stay steady. In fact, if it does not get any worse I might just live with it: a memory at the door of my head that I choose to imagine who it might be. In such ways writers are made. At least this one. *Entre vous.*

✕

Patsy had come out the Saturday of Ellen's death and cooked the teal so that each of us got a duck. She'd wrapped them in bacon and served them with carrots and potatoes from her garden, which was still producing, even with the recent snow. At dinner Buck raised his glass, but did not say "goodbye," instead saying something to himself. I had seen him do this before but could not lip-read to know what it was.

"The next time you shoot rabbits," said Monique, "I will make supper of them. In France it is a favorite meal, but their rabbits are domestic."

"It is *lapin* in French," I said. "Masculine."

"Good."

"The yard rabbits are mostly domestic," said Buck. "We used to save them for Moshe just to keep him busy."

"There's a brush pile down near the river with rabbits," I said. "Before you come out next time I'll shoot us two or three."

"*Deux, trois,*" Monique, said. And I repeated that. Then Buck asked, "What is the word for 'gun'?"

"*Fusil*," she said. "Masculine. I don't know the word for 'shotgun' if there is one." Then, to me: "That's plenty of *mots* for *toi* today, but don't think you can skip *demain*. 'Words' and 'tomorrow.' And *tu* and *toi* are French for 'you' when you are intimate. And while we are there, my term of endearment for *toi* is *mon chou*."

"What does that mean?"

"My 'cream puff'—*chou à la crème*—unless you'd rather be a 'cabbage.'"

"I'll take 'cream puff,'" I said.

"Can I be the cabbage?" said Buck. "I like cabbage."

"Yes, and you can even be a *tu*, because that includes family members."

"Good thinking," said Buck.

Over dinner we laid plans for the Colloquy. Monique wanted us each to pick a topic. She had picked *The Fall of the Cowboy* by Remington since Buck had it framed on the wall. The Ranch Doctor had told her he'd talk about an organ but had not decided which one. He'd bring illustrations. That left me, Buck, and Patsy. I said I'd talk about Andy Adams's *Log of a Cowboy* because I was in debt to it for something I had written and, as I had extra copies, I'd pass them around.

"I'll do pagans," Buck said.

"Pagans?" I didn't remember Buck ever saying anything about pagans. "What do you know about pagans?"

"I am one. That counts." Then he gave a short preface to his presentation, talking about Irish druids and how pagans don't have songs that go *Onward pagan soldiers, marching on to war, with the shells of turtles, going on before.*

"Is there something we should read about pagans?" I asked. I didn't get an answer because Patsy said she was going to talk about how Judas didn't hang himself from the Judas tree but got such a bad stomach from having betrayed Jesus that his belly split open and he spilled his guts into his vegetable garden, where they got plowed under, and how for forty years afterward it was known as the Blood Garden because it was an abundance of tomatoes. "Acts 18 to 20."

When we were back in my cabin, Monique said that for once Patsy had the Bible more or less right. And how in a way, it was like Milky for Patsy's garden, only that Milky did nothing bad. "All comparisons are dubious," she said. "Either Montaigne or Plato. I think Plato."

The next morning, Patsy fixed us One-Eyed Jacks early because Monique had to leave before noon in order to get home before dark; also Patsy wanted to get to Blaze to see Testy.

"We are going to read the passages from Acts," said Patsy, "where the folk are communists, and if you try to hide money from God that should go to the poor you get shot." Monique said that Patsy had gotten that more or less right as well.

※

When Monique drove down the lane, she turned her spotlight around so that it was aimed backward toward us. At the gate, before making a left on the Buckeye Road, she switched the light on and off a number of times until she reached the highway. It was her usual way of saying goodbye. Patsy followed her to the highway and Monique turned south, and Patsy north. We were getting some wind from the east as they left.

"Three days of wind from the east," Buck said, looking after Monique and Patsy as they drove down the Buckeye, "and we get rain. The guy who ran Half-Vast Ranch lived east from here and believed he could hear his dead wife's voice coming out of the verbena that grew down by the gate to the place. Crazy old goat. He thought he was Prince of Goa, whoever that is. He's pushing up soapweed now but I admired his madness. He was the last of the Prairie Populists. We need more like him in this country.

Maybe I'll hear Ellen's voice in the rain if it comes from the east." As in fact it would in three days, for three days. Walking to the kitchen, he asked how I thought I'd die.

"In my sleep," I said.

"'Death's second self that seals up all in rest,'" Buck said.

"Yes." I had left a copy of the Shakespeare poetry book we were using at school in the Home-House and apparently Buck had been reading it. He was a big reader, but never junk. Whatever I'd bring back from the Hays library, or some of the books I'd buy, he'd borrow to read. And it wouldn't be long afterward that he'd find some use in our talk for what he'd read. Sometimes it would be weeks or months later, but it would crop up. This time it was pretty recent. I had never thought about my death. It was a cliché answer. Buck called such answers "white bread." The reason they make white flour is because rats won't eat it, he'd say when Patsy would serve us her Wonder Bread sandwiches. He looked forward to Monique's bread.

"Do you think you'll go anywhere?" he asked.

"After I'm dead?"

"Yes."

"I don't know. That's what it means to be an agnostic," I said. "Not knowing. What about you?"

"Transmigration," he said. "Now that I know the word."

"You coming back around as yourself? Or coming back as a horse?"

"Snapping turtle food. That way you guys can't find me to make a fuss of the funeral. Make a guess for yourself."

"For me it might be like when Dorothy goes to Technicolor Oz and meets the folk from black-and-white Kansas," I said coming to the house. "'Transmigration' of fiction into fact—or the other way around."

"Ellen always thought she'd die on horseback," he said.

"Get thrown?"

"No. She thought she'd be riding in the back pastures beyond the tank on Charlene one day and just die. She thought she'd be old. But not too old to ride. She said she'd know in advance when the time would come, but wouldn't tell me."

"I never saw that kind of thinking in her," I said.

"I didn't either," Buck said.

"She told me that she looked forward to a life of cooking and tending a garden," I said. "Vegetables and flowers. Having friends over for meals. Good talk. Books to read."

"She'd tell me that as well," Buck said.

Sitting down at the kitchen table there was a pause between us, broken when Buck asked if I was going to write about us like I had once before. When I didn't answer, he said he'd learned from one of my schoolbooks that an elegy was poetry for the dead and a eulogy was prose.

"That's true." And nothing more was said.

That night he skipped his toast before supper. Nor did we tell a story of the scar, except Buck asking if I had one, and I said it could wait. And added: "Monique thinks she will die in France of the *nameless dread*, whatever that is."

"She told me that as well," said Buck. And then we were mostly quiet until I left for my cabin.

⋊⋉

Let death take me while I am indifferent to him. A mask may cover the rest of my life but in the last scene there is no room for pretense.
—Montaigne

In such ways does West Jesus Land, Kansas, find its way to me here in Paris. There are days, and this is one of them, when I wonder not only who I am, but where I am. Oddly, I rather like the feeling.

⋊⋉

The following week it got warm. The snow melted in the pastures quickly, and far into November the sky was clear. The Gomer was still marking the heifers. Some days you'd see three or four. Other days only one. You couldn't drive just one heifer, so if the herd was close to the yard, we'd rope her and lead her up to the corrals until there were others ready for the vet. Farther away, we'd hog-tie her in the bed of the pickup.

By the time the Ranch Doctor came out and we had our Colloquy, all that were going to get bred were bred, and we took the ones that weren't to the sale barn and returned the Gomer to Mencken.

After we loaded the bull into the stock trailer, I thought to untie the breeding collar. Over the summer it had lost its color, and we were finished with him.

"Don't bother," said Buck.

I was reaching through the opening on the side of the trailer near the front and almost had it off. That's when he rattled his horns. I took a hit in my right hand.

"Damn it," I said. I wasn't as gifted at swearing as Buck.

"You okay?"

"I think so." I looked at my hand: it was not punctured, but the Gomer's horn had knocked it against the side of the stock trailer. It was skinned raw on the backside, but that was about all. It would be black and blue by morning.

"Best to leave bent-peckered bulls alone," said Buck. "All bulls for that matter." We took the Gomer over to Cody's where we off-loaded him into a corral.

"How'd he do for you, Buck?" asked Mencken.

"Only three didn't get bred. We lost those two in the Saline from quicksand."

"Thanks for calling about that," Mencken said. "It's a bad way to go."

"Know any good ways?" said Buck.

"By your lonesome," said Mencken.

The following Friday the Ranch Doctor came out from Kansas City, picking up Monique in Lawrence where he had a holistic clinic. They arrived late, but Patsy had waited supper: buffalo chili over twice-baked potatoes and a big salad.

The next morning we had our physicals, rudimentary to be sure, but at least the Ranch Doctor put a stethoscope on us, hit our knees with the little arrow-headed hammer, pounded us on the back and chest with two fingers, looked in our ears and down our throats and—very important—grabbed our livers. Patsy had made it clear he couldn't pry into her privates "where the moon don't shine."

All was pretty much the same except I noticed that the Ranch Doctor did not as usual advise Buck to quit smoking, the advice being a routine joke between them because Buck had stopped years before. Monique had gotten her physical at the Ranch Doctor's clinic in Lawrence, which was why they were late. "She's as 'healthy as a fertile hog,'" the Ranch Doctor observed—not that we thought he knew anything about the health of hogs.

"But better looking to be sure," he added.

"Thanks be to that," said Buck.

Earlier that week, I had shot *quatre lapins* out of the brush pile by the Saline. I cleaned and skinned them to hang in the well house. By the time the Ranch Doctor and Monique got to the Home-House it was getting late, and so Testy had fixed us in advance a platter of doves with rice. Better to put off the rabbits until the next day.

We had supper in the Whorehouse Room and the Ranch Doctor told his version of the Scar, it being that it was like the life-line on your palm, but in the case of the Scar, you could see your fate by running your eye along it from Buck's end to where nobody sat just below the picture of the Dodge City Cowboy Band, and somewhere along the line you'd feel the power of life start to give out, and somewhere just past that you'd blink, and that was your fate.

I could have taken it the way I took Patsy's vision of the End-Time, but I did not. I noticed Buck seemed to be running his eye down the table toward the empty chair. I looked away so as not to see if he blinked.

After supper we had our Colloquy: First, Patsy made a cheerful presentation of the End-Time with all her grim details of the world on fire from flying Frisbees of shit, barbequed body parts, the Anti-Christ going the wrong way, but finally the joy of joining the real Jesus-God on his body at last. The only change from her previous predictions was that at the last minute she was going to grab me, Buck, and Monique by the hair and haul us along. The Ranch Doctor could fend for himself.

Monique took *The Fall of the Cowboy* off the wall and propped it on the music stand. Patsy wanted to know why it was called *The Fall of the Cowboy*, because the man standing by his horse had clearly not fallen off but gotten off. Monique asked Buck if he knew the answer, and in this way Monique did not have to do much explaining of the painting, but only ask us questions to which we gave answers, the first being from Buck: that its title was exactly right because the man had gotten off his horse to open a gate, and thus the West was now fenced off. From that point on, we all talked about the painting, with Monique getting us to understand perspective and how cold the painting was because of the pigments Remington had used, and the quality of his brushstrokes.

"*Coups de pinceau* is what they are called in French," she said. "Brushstrokes are to a painter what words are to a writer."

After about half an hour, Buck said we needed a break, and we all poured ourselves another drink. I stayed with wine, as did Monique, and the Ranch Doctor went back to whiskey along with Buck. Patsy got a bottle of La Belle Dame sans Merci she had been saving. Before the Ranch Doctor and Buck made their presentations, Monique played the piano, singing a version of "Old

Paint": *I ride an old paint, I lead an old Dan, I'm goin' to Montan'* *for to throw the houlihan.*

When it came his turn, the Ranch Doctor told us more than we wanted to know about the spleen, saying that when he was a young man he had first been a medical illustrator and the spleen was his favorite organ.

Somehow he had no ability to make the spleen interesting even though he knew more about his subject than the rest of us knew about ours. Mine was *The Log of a Cowboy*, a novel by Andy Adams that I thought was nonfiction until he had his cattle drive from Texas to Montana go through a bog in Western Kansas at Buck's ranch—where there was no bog.

Finally, it was Buck's turn:

"To be a pagan means what comes around goes around. Life is eternal, but to my mind not the way Patsy thinks it is. You feed yourself to the birds in the sky through a tree or grass going to seed on the ground, or you feed yourself to fishes and the turtles in the pond and you're part of life everlasting—even if it isn't yours. I don't see what difference it makes whose life it is, just as long as it's life. The fire ants got Moshe and that was fine by Moshe when he was dead and fine by the fire ants when they were alive. Milky is growing tomatoes and lettuce and carrots and potatoes in Patsy's garden and that is fine by us when we have salads or stews, and it is fine by Milky, who died for a good cause the way she lived for one. And that will be fine by me when I get past blinking down the Scar. Just like Uncle Sol, who started a worm farm in one of Leo's poetry books he left around here when he was teaching school."

Here Buck raised his glass and observed that goodbye has two syllables and so two meanings. Patsy asked who Milky was.

Later that night I woke up and could not go back to sleep, so I put on my clothes and walked over to Buck's. Monique was still asleep. Patsy had gone back to Hays, and the Ranch Doctor was going to stay over in her room. Through the window into the Whorehouse Room I could see Buck talking to the Ranch Doctor. I decided not to go in, and when I went back to the cabin, Monique woke up.

"Is there anything wrong?" she asked.

"I think so," I said.

The next day they left early for Lawrence and Kansas City after the Ranch Doctor shot some early mallards that were starting to come down. Buck took him and I stayed in the cabin with Monique. We did not talk about much as she packed. I asked her if she'd like to take a rabbit back. And what it felt like to be "healthy as a hog."

"Keep them for the next time," she said, not answering the second question. I saw her looking out the Thin Man Window from the far end of our bed. I sensed something pensive in her. She put her travel bag on the floor and got closer to the window, as if to get a better view of the yard. Then: "You'll never get through the window if you eat too many *choux à la crème*." She smiled, but not at me.

"They're back," she said, and, picking up her bag, followed me down the stairs and out the front door. Without her truck, I knew she would not be able to flash her spotlight goodbye. Still, I had sent her a postcard two days before.

Monique spent Thanksgiving with her parents in Kansas City, and then went to Paris over Christmas and New Year's to visit the family where she had stayed when she was a student. She invited me to go along, but I needed to be with Buck and the herd. It would have been my first trip outside the United States. And her invitation seemed tentative.

✵

As well as copying previous writers on Paris, I have decided to let the character of mine who lives with me describe it for both of us. If his voice sounds familiar then it follows that imitation is indeed a sincere form of flattery.

I live in Paris. I work for the English-language magazine France. We recycle articles about France from other magazines: "Gaillac, the Oldest Wine"; "Elizabeth David: The English Writer on French Cookery"; "Château de Mauriac Opens as Museum"; "Balzac's Paris." That kind of thing.

Our subscribers are the English and Americans who have settled in France and who don't read much French. Some are here in Paris, but mostly they are in the South of France, Provence and the Dordogne. The Ardèche. Pyrénées-Orientales.

We have a back page titled "La Résolution" that is a récit about France: sometimes about confusion à propos language; other times about farewells, bittersweet or otherwise. I am the writer of "La Résolution," a task that is pleasing for me in an ironic way, because while I believe in "La Fin," I do not believe in "resolutions"—either French or English. When I write "La Résolution," I write in order not to reveal myself. In so doing I am not always true to the facts. It is from these duties I am taking a week off to start this diary.

I have never married. I suppose that a single man, fully and pleasantly employed, with a long lease on a furnished apartment in the 7th Arrondissement, and with a decent palate for vins fins, must be in search of a wife. But I am not.

My apartment is a fifth-floor walk-up on Rue de Poitiers not far from the Musée d'Orsay. From here I have a cubist view of mansard rooftops and photogenic rues. I can see today's bird market on the Quai du Louvre. I can see Montmartre, or rather half of the dome of Sacré-Coeur, rather like a slice of moon in a Chagall. At night the lights from tourist boats that head up and down the Seine blaze through my windows, creating a Strobe-Light Disco Starry Night. I am not so high up that I don't hear street noises. And with the windows open smell the chestnuts roasted by the small old Moroccan man just across the street. It is all pleasant and pleasing in ways that I cannot explain, even to myself. Perhaps especially to myself—if that is what I am doing.

In summer, Paris gets hot and crowded: but I don't much mind.

*I rather like the city when it is filled with a plethora of Mr. and Mrs.
Bridges standing in front of the Grand Palais asking directions to
the Grand Palais. In winter, the city is not all that cold compared to
Kansas winters, and you can again walk in the smaller streets for
decent stretches before a taxi honks you off.*

*And I like the rain. I like coming into my restaurants and cafés
and brasseries to get warm and to be recognized. I think the reason
I have never married—or even had more than a series of pleasant
affairs (and in recent years only with wives who love their hus-
bands)—is because my affection for Paris is persistent, consuming,
and easy. When I am tired of it, I shall be tired of life.*

In all this my doppelgänger speaks for me. And he seems to
have learned his French from Monique as well as art history.

⚭

"The television is calling for snow," Patsy said after Monique and
the Ranch Doctor drove away.

"How much?" said Buck.

"Ten inches and wind."

"You want to stay?" I asked Patsy.

We had walked toward the cut through the shelterbelt on the
northwest side. From there you could see over the breaks into the
Saline and beyond. You could see the northern sky, and the western one as well. This time of year the snow came from the north;
early snows, like the one in October, came from the southwest. As
did spring blizzards. Patsy and I walked behind Buck, and when
we came out of the cut-through we saw low dark clouds proceed
by a deep blue line.

"How much?" said Buck again.

"Ten," Patsy said. "Maybe twenty."

"Cold?"

"The television said about the snow and wind, I didn't hear
about the cold," Patsy said.

"It looks to be cold. You better get to Hays if you're going," Buck said to Patsy.

"I'm staying."

Here's what happened: The heifers started calving in the blizzard, and we had to bring them up to stalls when we could; some of the calves froze when the heifers dropped them in the snow. Some of the heifers died as well. Others we didn't find until the spring thaw deep into the horse back pasture where sometimes we find a calf or two, but those were "cold burnt" and would never put on any weight.

There were days when the snow was too thick and the wind too hard for me and Buck to keep track of each other. After getting badly separated toward one evening and taking half an hour to find one another, then another half an hour to get back to the yard, Buck got out his father's .45 Army Colt and Patsy let me use her .22. In this way we would fire off a round to signal where we were. Up in the yard, Patsy would blast away with my shotgun every hour on the hour so we knew where she was. We did that for about a week.

Once I ran a heifer and her calf ahead of me toward the yard and then could only see the heifer and went back and found the calf and roped her. I hoisted her over the front of the saddle and rode back that way, following Buck's pistol shots.

Patsy ran a rope line from the Home-House to the calving stall so we could get back and forth without losing our way. We kept the horses up with the calves, all except Angel, who could not be caught and was not found later no matter where I looked when spring came. Mencken Cody said he'd seen her in the snow near Blaze, first running with the wind, then into it, kicking up her heels and whinnying like something possessed.

After the storm passed we began to count the dead in the herd. Given what we'd brought up to the yard and calved out, we'd lost half of everything. Some nights I thought I could hear a heifer bawling in the distance, mostly north of the yard, but when I'd ride out the next day, I'd find no tracks. *Ghost cattle*, Buck would say, confessing he'd hear the same thing.

It was March before there was more ground to see in the pastures than snow. A Robert Sudlow painting.

Despite our troubles, at the end of the day, with our whiskey, *Maybe her family will tell you where she is*, would come back to me. But as I would learn, they would not know themselves for many years, and by the time I got to Paris she was yet to be found.

After it was over we didn't get out for a month, except near the end to horseback Patsy to the highway, me on Chief leading Patsy on Charlene.

At the start, the wind took the phone lines down; the roads were drifted in after two days; we lost our electricity after the third day. It was a week after Patsy left before we got any mail, in my case the Pont des Arts postcard.

"What you got, Leo?" Mencken Cody said when he saw us off our horses on the edge of the highway to Hays. The road was clear but packed, and the most trouble we had was getting through the snow that the state had plowed into a drift. Mencken was the first one to come along.

"Patsy needs to get to town. And I need some food. You just get out?"

"Yes," Mencken said.

I tied the horses to a stop sign and we went to Hays, after which Mencken gave me a ride back and Patsy stayed at her place until we could get the lane cleared.

"Any whiskey in those gunnysacks?" Mencken said as he let me off coming back.

"Only buttermilk," I said, tying two sacks over Charlene's saddle and one to my horn.

"I'll believe that when Testy's Jesus-God comes flying by," Mencken said.

I followed my trail through the snow home, ponying Charlene. It was getting dark. And it had started to snow and blow again. I was blue-steel cold when I got there.

"Goodbye," I said to Buck as I tipped my Black Jack toward him.

"Blood's not meant for antifreeze," he said.

）（

Our affair had no other end than itself. It referred to nothing outside itself. It had neither one reason nor two, nor thousands. We kept back from one another. We loved because of who we were to one another.
—Montaigne, "A Friend I Cannot Find Again"

Montaigne is my shade, my scrim, and my light from five hundred years ago. Is it Monique who understood this would be true?

I am still in Paris but soon may leave and go south, for what reason I do not know. An impression to be true to. It snowed here for two days, then stopped. Memory triggered by weather.

）（

Coming out of Buck's one summer day to ask Patsy if she needed anything in town, I saw her lying on her back in the chicken moat. Her eyes were closed; chickens were walking around and flapping themselves over her. She was talking to herself. Not gibberish. Her hatchet was in her right hand and, as I watched, she raised it, the blade pointed first south, then west, then east, then north, all the time talking. Finally, she turned the blade to the sky and shook it, still talking. As she is alive, and might someday recover enough to read this, I am not going to write what I heard her say, except that it was a benediction for all of us I have included here.

Late in March we caught an ice storm, then snow fell on top of the ice, then a rain froze on top of the snow so that the pastures were crusted. Buck and I stood at the north edge of the shelterbelt from where we could see down toward the pond. We had moved what was left of the herd into the big yard, where the heifers (now cows) and their calves were milling among the houses and the sheds.

The sun was out. It was getting to be a warm afternoon. To the west was higher ground, and the pastures there ran downhill toward the pond. In some places there were small waterways, and it was from those waterways that we heard a sound, faint to be sure, but distinct. And farther down we could see water emerge from beneath the snow, breaking into the open for a stretch, then flowing again under the crust.

We stood there listening, and watching the sun lower itself, tossing shadows from the distant trees in the west toward Patsy's trail road and stock tank painted in the air, the edges becoming a mystery of their own making.

Instead of ringing the bell for supper, Patsy joined us, and the three of us watched the shelves of ice and snow collapse into the small streams they themselves had created. For no special reason we could name, we ate at the Scar Table that night but said little.

It was later that spring that Buck was not to be found one morning in the Home-House and Patsy came over to my cabin to say he was missing.

Canyon Snip was in the pasture, as were the other horses. The truck was there. In fact Patsy and I used it to drive around the boundary of the ranch and even over to Cody's place. We called into town and asked the sheriff to help us. Mencken Cody came over to help. A week of days and nights later we gave up, although I did ride Chief deep into the rattlesnake pastures and down to the Saline.

At the end, Mencken Cody stopped by and the three of us stood in the yard and talked about Buck and what he had been to us. We talked about how he had vanished and wondered why. And why he did not want us to know where he had taken himself. We talked about many other matters as well that I shall not write about here, except to note that Patsy went into the Home-House and brought out whiskey and three glasses, and we raised them in honor of Buck, and one by one said *goodbye.*

One Art

I majored in English at the university and one of my teachers showed me the Elizabeth Bishop poem that begins "*The art of losing is not hard to master.*" I thought so well of the poem I put it to memory, but now with mostly memory as my life (plus tinnitus knocking at my door), I have lost the poem as well as much else. That said, I am going to give it a try, the second line being: "*Lose something every day.*" I know the feeling. Maybe I should stop there.

Monique's second winter at the ranch, Buck said the pond was frozen solid, so Monique and I might like to skate on it, which we did. After a while we skated to the raft and sat there for a rest. Monique reviewed my French and added some more: snow (*neige*), pond (*l'étang*), ice (*glace*), very cold (*très froid*)—that, I knew—and the name for the small bottle of liquor she had by *bonne chance* brought out that weekend, and which we drank: *eau de vie.* I asked if she knew the word for "raft." She did not but said she'd look it up; in the meantime, boat was *bateau.* It was June before I thought to check the pond to see how the raft had made it through the winter. Sometimes the ice would twist it, and in so doing buckle the planks that made the top. One time it had lost a barrel. Instead of either driving down or riding Chief, I walked. Now and then that was what Monique and I had done, walk, and on the way back she would pick prairie flowers for a bouquet.

When I got to the pond I saw the south wind had blown the raft north and beached it on the slope of the dam. I wondered how this could have happened, because the engine block I used for an anchor was connected to the raft with a log chain, which we secured to the raft by running it through a large U-bolt Buck had salvaged from a dead tractor. When I got to the raft, there was no log chain, and no engine block, but the U-bolt was attached and sturdy.

X

Today's mail brought the news that my editor will not, after all, be coming to Paris, as she is getting married. Thank you, Aristotle, for a real-life Deus ex machina.

And a much delayed letter from Monique's mother telling me that when Monique left Paris, she went to the Dordogne with her husband and their daughter. But that was some time ago. She said Monique was not well. An impression that had been like the ringing in my ears for weeks now.

X

The Dordogne, Southwestern France

The sheep have been through the hay meadows in recent weeks. Dominique and his herders drive them in a round-robin route of about twenty kilometers, staying two or three days in each meadow. My guess is there are three hundred, including goats. They were below me for two days, the ewes giving birth, so that they are growing the flock as it moves. Now they are west of me, past the village of Saint-Philippe; I see them on my way to the Monday market in Castillon.

I live and write these days in a small stone house high in a vineyard. From my bedroom window at a distance I see the castle of Monique's Montaigne. It is more than sufficiently large for royalty. Very close by and out the same window is the wreck of the Château de Montagne (with a missing *i*), lived in by a *très difficile* countess who had her fingers broken last year by robbers (one at a time, according to the story going up and down the *côte*) until she produced the keys to her safe. Montaigne would not have believed it had he seen it himself. We are a country of stories. And skeptics. I am both.

I have been here a year by now and what has kept me from

63

writing, as before in Paris, I cannot say. But at least I know I have been kept from it. Nor do I share my *petite maison* with anyone. Nor have I found Monique.

I type in the mornings unless I go to the Monday market in Castillon, where, after my shopping, I take *le plat du jour* with friends at the Hôtel des Voyageurs—famous for its blood sausage and excellent *vin de pays*. Food is dear, but wine is inexpensive, at least for the *vin en vrac* that I buy from Monsieur R. I stop by his *chais* to fill my four-liter jug and gossip in my weak French, which is now augmented by Madame F., a neighbor just down the road, who is teaching me, but her lessons will sometimes overlap with Monique's. There is more than a little charm in the coincidence.

Afternoons I cut logs, clear brush, and help with the sheep at a small farm not far from me. In exchange, I am offered meals and wood for my stove. I walk to work, as it is only five kilometers. I move my feet to move my words.

I may become a father: the farm had six of its sheep killed by a mad dog. One of the ewes had just given birth, so we saved the lamb (now named Molly). Because I carried her into the house and laid her by the fire bright, she thinks I am her mother and follows me everywhere, bleating, bleating for her bottle. I don't have a place for her, but I might rig one. We'll see.

The hunters are busy these days, shooting from early in the morning until sunset: pheasants, *colombes* (a dove-like bird that migrates through on its way to Africa), wild boars, and small deer with a high-pitched bark.

I see these men by the sides of the roads that wind through the hills, sometimes with dogs. The other day one of them blew a brass horn as I passed. I do not know if he was calling something, or calling to other hunters that something was heading their way.

I have been trying to compost cheese rinds, eggshells, wilted lettuce, apple and pear cores, and bits of old pâté among other odds and ends in the woods between my house and the Château de Montagne. I seem instead to be feeding Boris—*mon sanglier*, a boar with an indiscriminate palate. Not that I have seen Boris eating the scraps, only that there are never any leavings from what I put out. Called to the hunters' horns or routed by their dogs, he would be fair game—and no doubt make a hearty ragout. Now that I have named him, I hope not. And he might be Borita.

A few days ago, a hunter brought a hindquarter of deer to the family that has Molly. The *femme de la fermière* used her butcher knife to carve the evening meal—and then some. Two sheepdogs shared the bones. I was invited to stay. My host opened bottles from his best years.

"There was a saying on the Kansas frontier," I said by way of a toast, "that the men were so hungry when they came in from the roundups, that the women fed the dogs first."

As my friends have learned that I once worked on a ranch, I am known as "Cue Boy," and in that guise I am expected to offer *bon mots* from the American West. We raise our glasses.

A great storm of wind and rain has come and gone, and now it is clear—although I have learned by the French radio (I do not have television—or Internet) that it will get *très froid*. So be it: I have a woodstove, blankets, and wool sweaters.

⋊

I Have Not

Madame F., an eighty-year-old American ex-pat from California who lives beyond a line of poplars down the hill from me, fell leaving my house after dinner the other night and hurt herself badly: a nasty twisting of bones and cartilage in her left foot and lower leg. I got help from neighbors and we took her to the hospital in Libourne.

The French medical system is excellent; true, it is in a high fever of fiscal misery these days, but I sense the French think it is better to be in debt to themselves for their own care than to China for television sets, or to the Middle East for oil and war.

After a few days, Madame was taken (not sent) home in a hospital van. Medical attention continues: visits by a nurse a few times a week, a doctor less often, but routinely—or as needed. Of course there are her friends. Me among them.

In the mornings I start her woodstove, a long arrangement of cook ovens, griddle plates, burner tops, and water reservoirs that not only heats her ancient mill of a house but cooks the meals she makes for all of us who have been her guests. Evenings I walk her dog, Ginger, a tall Rhodesian Ridgeback who sits partway into the large fireplace in the evenings because, out of her country, she is cold.

My neighbor and I talk books: Russian stories we read together in the early fall, and now de Maupassant: "Boule de Suif," which made him famous; "The Story of a Farm Girl"; and "Madame Tellier's Establishment." (We have agreed *not* to reread "The Necklace" in protest, but of what we are not sure.) I have introduced her to the American western writers Andy Adams and A. B. Guthrie.

In between the Russians, the French and the Americans, we confess our literary prejudices and affections: How much better Carlyle is as a writer on the French Revolution (even if wrong) than Dickens (even though he dedicated *Hard Times* to Carlyle). The splendor of Chekhov. And Montaigne, that I am challenged by Madame to read in French but cannot do, so instead try a paragraph here and there, only to return to the translation I bought for myself, not telling Monique should I find her here.

Finally, our admiration for Willa Cather in spite of Mencken's remark, that "of course she writes beautifully but who wants to read about Nebraska."

"The same could be said of you, Leo," Madame said, "and Kansas." I was too flattered to respond. How she knows of me in that regard, I have not asked. But once she said: "I alone know."

We also talk about the death of Alain Robbe-Grillet and the novels of Duras (and while we are there, the wine by the same name). How neither of us have read Radiguet. All this, and whatever comes from our mutual reading of the *Guardian* or the *New York Review of Books* (she subscribes to both), and the *International Herald Tribune* (my subscription forwarded down from Paris)— along with other literary journals and belles-lettres magazines we share with one another, and with those in our circle, some carrying stories of mine published under a pseudonym. Old and gray and lovely by the fire, my friend is a delight. I wonder if she knows my stories when she reads them. I think she must, but it is her charm not to ask me about them.

The other evening she asked if I have met the *jeune femme* French American who this past summer moved into a farmhouse at L'Étang on the Montaigne estate; she is a painter. *Très belle:* I have not.

"She was here when she was a girl, living with her mother and father also at L'Étang in the summers, coming down from Paris," said Madame. "But then one summer they did not return. She has grown into quite a beauty, like her mother. She has just returned."

Madame confessed that she had asked her to do the Monday morning market shopping. She thanked me for bringing in wood from the sheds below the house and building and stoking the fire, for walking Ginger—but the market needs a woman's touch. And no doubt better French, not confusing *rougette* (a small reddish lettuce) with *rouget* (a large reddish fish). Then there was the matter of *aiguilles*, which I understood to be sewing needles but were in the market patois *aiguillettes*, thin strips of meat; sewing needles cannot, as it turns out, be sautéed with garlic in olive oil. Nor can lettuce be poached with lemon and Herbes de Provence.

Perhaps, Madame suggested, the three of us could read

Radiguet (in French) and talk about it over dinner one night. In French. It does not seem possible for me, but I do not say so. Nor do I confess my desire to meet the French American *jeune femme*.

Accept the fluster of lost keys, an hour badly spent.
The art of losing isn't hard to master.

I started back in on "One Art" when I first got here and realized that my teacher had told me it was a villanelle (in Italian, "a small room"). "And thus form informs memory," she continued. "Like rhyme." I think I need to start over, go backward in my head, or round and round in it, to see if in my mind's eye I can find a small room of a poem.

I Am to Be a Godfather

It has been decided I am to be a godfather to Molly with visiting rights. It seems best she stay with the flock, as she has made friends with the other young lambs—three sets of twins among them—and that is fine by her and by me. In the evenings, I prepare her bottle, and when she hears me come out of the house into which I first carried her, she bounds up the rows of vines to bleat me a greeting. I know it is not love, but the bottle I carry that is love. French folk and flock are not confused—or conflicted—about such matters. We understand I will not take her home but might, if the weather turns foul, carry her to the fireplace where she was first warm.

Tomorrow to the Saturday-morning market in Sainte-Foy-la-Grande for myself, and to get a wedge of old *fromage de brebis* (I can't make a mistake about that) for my broken-footed friend. Cold again tonight. Maybe a nip of Armagnac. Maybe more than a nip.

Some Wines Are at Home in a Pichet

My house sits at the *carrefour* of four wine districts. West is

Saint-Émilion, one of the great wine regions of France. I own a few bottles; my friends gossip I am saving them for my *lit de mort*. Some French think it is better to drink the good wines young: my prized Saint-Émilions included. I'll split the difference one winter night over a good cut of veal. And Saint Agur. Or maybe a meal with Madame when she is well enough to return to my table. The future is a promise you keep to yourself.

Across the Dordogne River (about ten kilometers south) is Entre-Deux-Mers—where they make a light, white wine that I am told does not travel but is splendid here in summer. Or with *truite de mer* anytime. Crisp. Dry. To the north a kilometer or two is the Côtes de Francs region. I can see the vines from my second-floor windows. It is good wine and a good value. There is something tough and lean about it. In winter, it gets better if you open it and put the bottle by the woodstove thirty minutes before dinner. I drink half a bottle one night, then the other half the following night. Sometimes I fail at this arrangement.

The vineyard that surrounds me is the Côtes de Castillon. It is those vines that produce Château Perreau Bel-Air, a wine I will serve to visitors from America should I have any. Looking out the French doors in my dining room they will be able to see what they are drinking. Our toast will be to tip our glasses to the vines. None of this is about to happen.

East five kilometers is Bergerac, with vineyards that make a sturdy, dependable red wine. Monsieur R. resents the upscale vintners who are making Bergerac a Bordeaux-styled wine so that it might be exported and sold at rich prices. "Some wines are at home in a *pichet*," he said. "That way, 'if it gets broken at the table, desire shall not fail.' Confucius."

Monsieur is a *chais* of aphorisms. He is roughly the age of Madame F., and they are *chers amis*. He, too, is helping with her these days.

I didn't catch Monsieur's meaning, but he seemed pleased with himself for his saying, which he repeated while he filled my jug. The wine—a *mélange* from his scattered small vineyards of various appellations—is strictly illegal, and that pleased him as well.

One of his vineyards is not far from where *la nouvelle américaine* (as Monsieur calls her) lives. Between Madame and Monsieur her full name will become "Mademoiselle Nouvelle Américaine."

"*Très nouvelle*," said Monsieur. "A young *tête sur les jeunes* shoulders', to quote Catullus."

From time to time I have seen her driving the roads in an *ancien* blue Dyane truck with potted flowers painted (by her?) on the doors. She zips by with such speed and apparent determination to get where she is going that I cannot get a good look at her. I doubt she sees me at all. Because I drive a maroon Deux Chevaux made by the same company and about the same vintage, I thought one day to flash my lights as we passed: one *voiturette* to another. I got a quick flash in return.

I told Monsieur that all I could remember from Catullus was "What a woman says, you can write on the wind, write on the rushing waves."

"*Ah oui*," said Monsieur. "But wind and waves are lovely, and it is better to have a *faux récit* than *rien*. Far better, as Cicero says. And a man has well lived his life if he drinks the last bottle from his cellar on his last day," he continued as he corked my jug. Walking me to my Deux Chevaux he quoted Shakespeare, saying that a young man should be whipped who plays at being a connoisseur of wine and sauces.

"It was Montaigne who wrote that about young men and wine," Madame told me when we were talking of Duras and Radiguet. "Not Shakespeare. He gets many things wrong, and I think it is on purpose. Either that or he is finally addled."

I asked her about the "broken pitcher at the table," and she said she believed it might be the Old Testament but is badly quoted, and had nothing to do with wine. She would look one day. I decided not to mention Cicero or Catullus. In this, as with my talk in Kansas, some things do get said.

Gray Is the Color of the Dordogne Sky

Gray is the color of the Dordogne sky this time of year. Sometimes with streaks of red or pink as the sun tries to burn its way through. The other day nothing got through because of a deep fog that came in the night. When I walked down to start Madame's fire, the spider webs from summer were wisps of tendrils, white with the frozen frost. As I passed, they moved as if shivering. There was both the shade as well as the substance of things.

The vines and the wires on which they are strung were a dark brown, speckled with the white of the frozen fog. The grass in the pasture and the few large, round hay bales left from the fall mowing looked a pale yellow covered by a thin white shawl. Ten meters from my friend's house I could only make out its shape: no doors, no windows. It will be the same for my house when I walk up the hill, only wizened webs in the icy air and lines of brown vines making a perspective into the mist.

"Do you get fogs in Kansas?" Madame asked me as I loaded her stove. I told her not many, at least in the west where I lived. But we got blizzards. Big ones.

She was also curious about horizons. Madame said she understood that in Kansas you could see the edge of the earth in every direction. I told her this was true.

"In California," she said, "where I lived when I was a student, you could see the edge of the earth over the sea. Here we do not have a horizon. At least I never think of it with all the trees and the hills."

She seemed to study something in her mind, and I wondered if it was a recovered vision of the sea—or if she was trying to imagine the vast sweep of High Plains pastures with their circle of horizons that is my own recovered vision these days.

When the fog cleared (two days' worth), it was such a lifting of gray that I saw the landscape as if for the first time. There were other, albeit muted, colors: dark evergreens among the brown and gray trees; trunks of the oaks and chestnuts with pale green-gray molds and lichens up and down their barks. In the winter's pale light moss is everywhere on the rocks and trees—not only on the north side as it is in Kansas. With evening the tree trunks and the tree limbs grow a Manet-black before all else. Large dark-green balls with dots of white (like Christmas decorations) appear in the trees after the leaves have fallen: mistletoe. It is not prized by the French, but is by the English in the area.

"We did not have much mistletoe where I lived in California," said Madame one day. "I expect you did not in Kansas either."

"Where I went to the university," I said, "there were trees along the rivers with many bunches high up." I told her how one year Monique and I made Christmas money by shooting into the mistletoe with a .22 rifle so that they splintered and I could collect the stems and berries when they fell. I did not tell her the rest of the story. Nor did she ask me about Monique.

"I recently read a short story about a man here who lived in Lamothe in the post office after the war who did that," Madame said. "A curious fellow with very poor but amusing French—as the author had him." She added, "Please don't teach these French that trick with the mistletoe. It will just make for more gunfire along the *côte*." Here she paused as if to ask a question about the story, but she did not. Maybe she knew.

Snoopy as the Red Baron

I am a father again: Noël, a ram this time, lost his mother a few days after she gave birth. Sometimes the ewes in this country die mysteriously, perhaps of a calcium deficiency, and we think that is what happened. Noël, like Molly, is now bottle fed three times a day. Two orphans together. We wonder if they will become friends.

They run to the farmhouse side by side to get their meals. Molly seems to bleat more; Noël is the serious one. I should not have favorites. Molly is my favorite.

Cold and damp in recent days. Cold is cold. Damp is damp. In the Dordogne, they add up to more than Cold and Damp. Because the bottom half of my house is built into a hillside it does not get warm in winter. My woodstove is in what used to be the fireplace upstairs. At the other end of the room is the bathtub. Only the kitchen and the dining room are downstairs. It is where I write this diary, the cursor on my computer screen in search of the next word. With my stocking hat and scarf I am a vision of Snoopy as the Red Baron.

I am thinking of returning to Paris for a few days. Paris is what makes me an American writer, and I need to visit it now and then to see if I am still there. It has been a while now since I arrived here, and it is the thought of going back to Paris that has me writing again. These days I go back and forth in different ways to find myself, plus another as well—though not yet successful in either search. I have put it badly; I will ask Monsieur R. if he has an aphorism I may borrow. Maybe consult my Montaigne, as I seem to be steeped in him. Or instead of returning myself, as the lease on the apartment is not yet up, I might have my roommate write me here. The transmigration of fiction into fiction. He is the kind of writer who might be amused by it.

Verb Tenses Matter

Madame asks what I *will* be writing. She is discreet enough not to ask what I *am* writing. Verb tenses matter in matters of literary decorum.

For lunch we are having *soupe éternelle*. At the Monday market I bought a sturdy wood-fired dark bread. If kept in a cold room it will last the week. In addition to the bread and soup there is the *vieux fromage de brebis* from Sainte-Foy-la-Grande and a *pichet de vin rouge* from Monsieur R. Ginger is partway in the fireplace. "Demain," Madame's cat, is curled on a wicker chair. I am at the stove.

"You don't need to say about your writing," she says. "If you are *superstitieux*. And for all I know, you may not be writing. "*Pas de tout.*"

My friend is also trying to improve my French, and she does this not only by using words I do not know, but cognates as well. In this way, like her predecessor, she is an excellent teacher; there are days when I walk home with a new word (or a previous one) in my head, repeating it as I go, until I get back to my *Larousse*.

"*Pinceau, pinceau, pinceau,*" I said to the vines walking home from Madame's: "*Pinceau, pinceau.*" Up the hill I walked and talked to the vines on my way past them: *coup de pinceau*. Piero della Francesca, we had observed the hour before, has lovely ones. For this I did not need my dictionary.

I tell Madame I am not *superstitieux* and that in answer to her question, I am keeping a diary that is a memoir.

"*Un mémoire méditatif?*" she asks.

"*Un récit méditatif,*" I say.

"Does your diary have dialogue?" she asks.

"Some," I say. "Among myself and others."

"Me included?"

"*Ah oui,*" I say. She is quiet for a moment. Then: "And in between our talking, what else is there?"

"It is being composed like a Montaigne essay," I say. "I am using his aphorisms, but not putting them in italics. I am in search of myself through my words. Some of them not my own. Many must do so. It is not fiction. There is little plot. Only..." and here I stop. And she looks at me for a moment.

Then: "*Pas d'intrigue!*" Madame says in mock alarm. "Will anyone in America read such a memoir? *Pas du tout!*" She smiles as I bring the soup to the table and pour the wine.

I decide not to tell her I am indeed *superstitieux*—but not about what she has asked, or how she has asked it. Nor do I tell her what I wrote in Paris before I came here. And some of what I wrote before being here that she has by chance read. For some reason I touch wood as I put down the soup.

"*Soupe éternelle, c'est nous*," says Madame. It is her traditional toast over her traditional soup. We tip our glasses toward one another. She seems amused that I could write a memoir bereft of readers. However, delicious pleasures when enjoyed by themselves don't need the world's touch. As we begin lunch she asks if I am just now keeping the diary or if I began it when I first came here.

"From before in Paris," I say.

"*C'est récent*," Madame says to teach me the phrase. "Unless it is very recent, then it is *c'est plus récent*. Which is it?"

"Both."

"Then it would be *les deux*."

"*Les deux*," I say.

"*Ah oui.*" She seems amused at not only her language lesson but at my confession.

"The soup," she says as we start our meal, "has *un supplément* by Mademoiselle Américaine. She was here yesterday and asked about you. She is curious as to where you were before, and why you are here—as are we all. Except Monsieur R., who will make it up without regard to the facts."

It is a rich soup: beans and rice, mixed with bits of both rabbit and chicken—pleasing enough, Madame and I think, to warrant a second glass of wine. And more bread to mop the plates clean.

"You should put French words into your *récit méditatif*," Madame continues. "Add a phrase or two: *et, peu à peu*, you will get the language. And in this way your book will make you." I have been told as much before, but do not say so.

She wonders why my French is not better, since I have lived in Paris.

"Too many people speak English," I say.

"*Ah oui.*" I sense she wants to ask why I lived in Paris before coming here, but does not. I like her for that: we are both true to our impressions about one another.

I walk off lunch on my way to Molly's, feeling snow in the air. When I get there, I rick the stove wood cut from the previous day, then cut long logs and stack them like tepee poles around straight trees. That done, Molly and Noël are to be fed (they remind me in not-so-subtle ways) before all is dusk, then dark.

I am invited to stay for dinner, but decline. I have a dish of my own making at home: a casserole of potatoes, carrots, onions, and *saucisse de canard* into which I will stir my unique *moutarde douce* sauce. There is also a glass of *eau de vie de prune* that I have promised myself for some reason I will fabricate along the way: Better a *fausse raison* than none.

As I walk along, the scent of snow that was in the air earlier becomes *le neige* before I remember she is *la neige*. I am to stop at Madame's to stoke her stove for the night. Getting there I see the blue Dyane in the driveway, and I see Mademoiselle walking toward the house: tall, a holly berry scarf around her neck. Black pea coat, its collar turned up. Jeans. Yellow stocking cap. As she goes in the door, the light from inside shines on her face. She is maybe half my years, even though I am not yet a man of a certain age.

A puff of smoke comes from Madame's chimney and I know all inside is well and warm. Before I head up the hill home, I study in the dim light the potted flowers painted on the side of Mademoiselle's truck: a mixture of geraniums, deep purple petunias, bright-eyed pansies, and a tiny orange flower I do not know. Cold as it is, there is a sturdy glow to them. "Audacious," I think, both the flowers to be out in the winter night, and to paint them on the side of the old truck. "Intrepid": I'll look them up.

Monsieur R.

Monsieur R. is French, but long ago he lived for a number of years in California where he worked in the movie business, and so he speaks excellent English. However, we have agreed that we will speak French in order that mine might improve.

But Monsieur's French slips into a stream of French and English, unbroken, as if he is speaking an integrated language—a patois that is richer and more fluent than Franglais. He seems not to notice this. Madame tells me he speaks that way to her as well, and the times he has joined us for a meal, I observe this is true.

Monsieur is also given to asserting the truth of matters that are not, strictly speaking, true. The other day as he was drawing my four liters of his *vin rouge* plus another five liters for Madame, he announced (apropos of nothing I could fathom) that "Jesus said *casseroles* should *pas* call kettles *noir.*" And later, in the same conversation, he quoted Montesquieu when he said that a man needs six hours of sleep, a woman seven, while a fool takes eight.

"You should hear what he does in the name of Cervantes and Brillat-Savarin," Madame says when I stop with her wine. "'A meal that does not end with cheese is like a pretty woman with a mustache.' It is not a 'mustache' but 'with one eye,' and it was not Sancho who said it, but Brillat-Savarin who wrote it. Oh well," she laughs. "And the way he quotes you!"

"Me?"

"Yes," she says. "And me as well. We are all *personnages* in his *oeuvre.*"

"Me?"

"*Ah oui!*" she says. "You have *une histoire* à *la Monsieur.* Complete with intrigue and dialogue. And plot. Aphorisms. He claims to know why you came here as I told you he would. And why you were in Paris years before. The other day he had you saying by way of explanation that 'there is no royal road to learning,' which I think comes from Dickens or Trollope. And in any case is not much of an explanation."

I said I remembered saying no such thing, but that I was pleased to be credited. But on the subject of my travels, I said nothing more.

"He quotes me as saying, 'Far-fetched and dear bought is not good for women,' which comes from where I don't know, but not from me," says Madame. "And he quoted Mademoiselle Améric-aine saying, 'Art is long but life is short,' which she might have said because it is an old saying; at least I have heard it before. Still it is not what someone young would say, even a painter. And I don't think they have met. But soon she, too, will have *une histoire*. No doubt entangled with yours. In the meantime, he is trying to decide if you are returning to what he calls Black-and-White-Kansas when summer comes, or if you are staying here in Technicolor France. You are in more than a *récit méditatif*, I assure you."

I am at Madame's sink bottling her wine when I notice something new over the fireplace: her portrait. Acrylic, I think. A pale gold background that sets off her white hair and against which her face is luminous. Her head is tilted right to left against the traditional line. Her eyes are rendered large and dark brown, but not enough to be piercing. The painting is beautifully composed and rich with underpainting. Madame is lovely in it, although likeness was probably not the object of the artist.

"I have no wrinkles," Madame says, when she finds me looking at it. "She put Botox on her palette. Her *coups de pinceau* are unique—*seul en son genre*. The same as in the potted flowers on the side of her truck. I like especially the orange 'million bells' because they are from pots of mine. Have you seen the flowers on her truck?"

I say I have: "*Intrépide*," I say.

"*Ah oui*," says Madame and smiles at my new word.

X

Castillon is the small market town where on Mondays I buy my fish and *fromage* and, from the tall Madagascar woman, the wood-fired bread that lasts a week.

After shopping, I take a *grand crème* at the Commerce Café with friends, also there for the Monday market. We gossip—mostly in English to accommodate my poor French—about the usual: weather, grapes, the price of gas, and the good lunches to be had next door at the Hôtel des Voyageurs, the home of Yu-Yu, a small parrot that does not like anybody very much, and me, it seems, in particular: always squawking with grating intensity when I come in.

"Before Yu-Yu there was Mal-Mal," says Monsieur R. "He had excellent French profanity. Some very good words."

The Hôtel des Voyageurs is a "ticket restaurant." In Castillon there are no Michelin stars. No Trip Advisor decals. A ticket sign on the door means it is for those who work in town and do not want to go home for lunch. In that case their employers have made arrangements for a meal: if you come back over and over again—a kind of *habitude*—you earn a discount on a future meal, or maybe the meal itself. I am not all that sure how it works. I should ask. Now that I think of it, I have seen such restaurants in Paris. At the Hôtel des Voyageurs you can get a three-course meal for eight euros. *Vin* included.

The restaurant has two rooms. They are divided by the kitchen, in which there is a fireplace that is used as a grill. The old vine stumps (*pieds de vigne*) that are pulled each winter from the vineyard below my house (and others all along the *côtes*) are bundled and sold for firewood. There are mathematical odds à la Diderot that the *côte de porc* I ate for lunch at the Hôtel des Voyageurs the other day had been cooked over the *pieds* that made the wine that was included in the meal.

As for the room behind the kitchen: I am not allowed. Once when I looked it was packed with men eating *ensemble* at a long wide wooden table. They were pouring the dregs of their wine into the dregs of their soup and drinking it out of the bowls; crusts of bread were scattered about, the men's spoons and forks making a *porte couteau* of the bread. From the front room we had heard the swarthy laughter of these men. I am not sure women are allowed. I am pretty sure they are not. I could see no scar running the length of the table, but my guess is there were stories nonetheless.

What Rat?

"Does she ask you to pee in her compost?" says Monsieur. We have arrived by chance at the same time to do chores for Madame and are walking her lane toward the house. Before I can answer Monsieur says: "Every cock will crow upon his own dunghill."

For a moment in my mind's eye I see Monsieur taking a pee on Madame's compost while crowing away. The vision passes and I say, no, she has not made such a request, although she has asked me to continue her compost while she is unable—a small square plot fenced off against Boris, should he get tired of my fare.

"Nor me," says Monsieur. "But Burton in his *Melancholy* writes that peeing into the compost makes it richer."

Monsieur is a tall man with large hands and long arms. He is older than I am, but the lope in his walk is younger than mine. There is a movie-actor visage about him, something beyond handsome or distinguished. No doubt he has broken many hearts.

"And what shall we do with the rat?" he asks. We are at the door, and without knocking, Monsieur walks in—not waiting for an answer from me, which would have been: *Quel rat?*

Monsieur has come this day to make croutons out of the bits of Madame's bread left over from the previous week, including the forked ends of the *baguettes serpentines* she has me buy. He takes great care in making his croutons, using sea salt, good garlic, and Spanish olive oil he gets from a friend near Seville who, Madame confides, may be a woman. *"Un peu d'intrigue—comme vous,"* she says. "And we do not know for sure he is married as he claims to be. I have never seen a wife. First, she was in California; then she is in Greece with her dying mother; recently she has come and gone from London. She is in Paris. She is in Belgrade. She is with a friend in Addis Ababa. I think he only says he is married so he won't be pressed to marry. This has been going on for years—even when he was in California. I would not marry him if he asked, so he has nothing to fear from me. And Countess P. will not have him in her house, so he need not worry about her."

It is Countess P. who lives in the Château de Montagne (with the missing *i*) and with—or without—broken fingers. I have never seen her, although it is said she drives out now and again in an ancient white Citroën. It is also said she is a direct descendant of General Talbot, the Englishman who finally lost the Hundred Years' War in the Cult (Protestant) Valley below the Catholic Côte. Up here she is out of her religion and said to be more than loony about it.

As to Madame's kitchen, I had wondered why there always seemed to be a large bowl of croutons on the kitchen counter. And when I thought of it, I should have wondered about other dishes that seemed to appear: Who had made the *potage Crécy* or the *saucisson* with horseradish sauce? Or the *potage bonne femme* (which became the base of my own *soupe éternelle*, now in weak competition with Mademoiselle Américaine's version). And who was leaving lovely apple tarts with thin, delicate crusts? Some from Monsieur, some from Mademoiselle, I have concluded. *Un peu d'intrique.*

"What is to be done with the rat?" says Monsieur from the counter where he is mixing the stale bread chunks in the iron skillet with its hot Spanish olive oil, garlic, sea salt and a concoction of spices.

"I think it best to take him to the Dordogne," says Madame. "Is he caught?" They are talking about a Ragondin rat for whom Madame had set a trap by her pond before she fell.

"He is not," says Monsieur. "But when he is, let me drown him in the trap. I take them to the Dordogne and they return and you catch them again; then, I take them to the Dordogne and they come back. Voltaire writes that 'man is born free but that everywhere he is like a rat in a trap.'"

"You have it wrong," says Madame. "It is that 'everywhere he is in chains': *dans les fers*. And it was Rousseau, not Voltaire."

"I take it," says Monsieur (and here he uses Madame's pet name, at which she blushes, so that he smiles with the youth that is his walk), "you would rather not have us say: 'How now? A rat? Dead, for a farthing.' And yes, he is caught."

"It's Shakespeare," she says, "and I doubt it's a farthing. But I thought you said the rat has not been caught."

"What difference does verb tense make?" says Monsieur. "'Will be caught,' 'has been caught,' 'is caught,' 'shall be caught.' Since the war and Camus, we are all *aujourd'hui c'est moi qui suis mort. Et le rat*, also!"

"No," says Madame (and here she uses a pet name for Monsieur at which he smiles toward me), "I do not want him dead. To the Dordogne. Swim, swim, vile rat, swim. And you don't know for sure the same rat returns."

"I'll mark him," Monsieur retorts. "Polka dots of orange water-resistant paint from a spray can I have in my Dyane. If Monsieur Ragondin comes back we will know. Then, Madame," and here he turns off his frying pan and scatters his croutons on a paper towel, "will you let me drown him? He would make excellent fertilizer for your tomato plants. I will cut him into pieces and put one piece per plant: a hindquarter here, the *tête* there, the butt end here. The innards there. A big Ragondin will feed half a dozen plants, and with ten tomatoes a plant that would be sixty tomatoes with ease that would grow round and red with vigor and abundance."

"The tomatoes will smell like rat."

"No more than your onions smell like pee."

"A dead rat stinks more than a living man's pee," she says.

"That's Ovid. Ovid said that."

"He did not," she says. "I said that."

"Well, then," Monsieur says, bringing his croutons to the table so we can taste test them, "let us talk about Countess P.'s tongue."

"What about her tongue?" says Madame.

"How the tip of it was cut off for the keys to her safe and now she talks gibberish."

"I hear she always talked gibberish to that Talbot shrine of hers," says Madame.

"She has a shrine?" I say.

"I think it's true, but I doubt it," says Monsieur.

The next afternoon when I go to the farm, I learn that Molly does not exactly remember me (how quickly they forget), but Noël does. And there is Sylvester.

Sylvester? Yes. His mother will have nothing to do with him: so now there are three. Bleats all around. And well, yes, Molly does remember me. Or something about me.

The Small Room Adds Furniture

Practice losing farther, faster
Places, names, and where it was you meant to go.
None of these will bring disaster.

Now there are tables and chairs and—all of a sudden—I find a watch and also houses and countries—or maybe cities. The poem's list is not a list but a room to be filled.

My Cork Basket Is Half Empty

I am more than halfway through winter. I know because the basket where I keep old corks is much depleted. There are many clocks that mark the seasons in the Dordogne. These days you can see the vineyard owners planting new vines. The shooting from hunters has stopped. Primrose is blooming. Paper whites are for sale in the markets. The daffodils that were planted up against the stone walls of the old houses and barns where the ground is warmer are coming up. V's of cranes are heading north. The wild plum trees between Countess P. and me are starting into bloom. And my cork basket is half empty.

I use the corks to start my woodstove. When I open a new bottle I try not to pierce the cork, so that I can turn it around for the wine I bottle from my jug. There is a curious pleasure in pulling a cork from a fine Saint-Émilion (only a few of these) and other corked (if not deeply punted) wines I buy. Twice pierced, the corks can no longer be used for rebottling Monsieur's wine but have other jobs: "double tasking," I have learned it is now called in America. "Triple tasking," now that I think of it. And *tant pis* for the prohibition against new wine in old bottles.

I save the spring-through-fall corks for winter fires. They are splendid starters (candle stubs are good as well) if you stuff a few in crumpled newspaper: I use the *International Herald Tribune* or, if I am feeling pretentiously French, *Le Monde*. Once the corks catch, they burn with great brilliance and flame. And kindle the wood into warmth.

The French Make Terrible Fences

The farmer where I feed Molly, Noël, and Sylvester has asked me to cut fence posts out of his woods. He, too, knows that spring is coming and his demand for firewood is not great, but he will need fence posts for a new corral I am to build around the sheep shed.

The French make terrible fences. Not even the most hard-scrabble Kansas ranch has such awful fences as most of the farms in France have. Both the posts (twisted and tilted) and the fence itself (drooping wires) are badly done. The gates are a wobbly wreck. They don't know how to make a brace post, or set a dead man. They don't see the need to make the gateposts bigger than the fence posts. I tell my neighbor that building and mending fences was one of the chores I had at the ranch, and I liked the pace of it: the way you look down a line of posts to see the end where you are going. And when you get there, watching the new wire pull tight as you stretch it against your brace post. Good thinking, as my rancher friend said when it was all done, new staples hammered in as well. Good thinking, he said: as well as: "*Are you going to marry Monique?*"

If there are not more pressing chores, I will show the owner how to build a proper fence. But it won't be easy. There are no fence stretchers to be bought or borrowed; the French fence wire is thin and of poor quality. They use bent nails for staples. But we'll see. In the meantime I am cutting the posts, plus extra wood for the fireplace should spring be false. For sure, I am going to build a sturdy and straight-lined corral, stout enough to hold a High Plains Gomer bull.

Yesterday from the woods where I was working I watched Mademoiselle drive up to the farmhouse and go in. She was wearing a bulky white sweater and the same stocking cap and holly berry scarf as when I first saw her. I turned off the chainsaw and thought to join her but did not. I am not shy. But something—not being covered with wood chips and that I no doubt reeked of work—stopped me. I sense a need to talk to her. But not with others around.

No Denouement

"And will there be a gun over the fireplace to go off before the end?" Madame is again curious about what I am writing. I tell her there are fireplaces, large enough for cold dogs to sit by on winter days, but no guns over them. Not yet in any case.

We have been reading Chekhov: Yalta is warmer than the

Dordogne this time of year. The pleasure in reading Chekhov is rereading him. There is no story we plan to boycott. Monsieur R. wants us to read *King Lear*, but Madame has resisted.

"He thinks the play is funny," she said. "However, what he quotes from it is accurate—at least by my memory. The other day he was here saying that 'age is necessary,' and sure enough, after he left I found it. I suppose that is amusing in a way, but I am not in a good enough mood to be amused by *King Lear*."

It occurs to me that Monsieur has never asked what I do or why I am living here. When first we met, he seemed to assume I had been in my small house on the hill for as long as he had been in his assortment of stone barns and buildings and *chais*. Or as long as Madame in her converted mill. None of it true of course, as by gossip he surely knew.

And further, it was as if we had all been in California together, whenever that was. Not that I know that Monsieur and Madame knew one another in California, but there was that remark she made about Monsieur's *fausse épouse* in California.

It is also true that Madame has never asked what brought me here, or why I have stayed. Or why I am alone. She may be shy about asking. I think this is true. I would be shy about telling her. I think that in asking about my writing she is asking about my life. She is right to do so.

"Will there be a curtain that hangs?" asks Madame.

I say so far there is no curtain. A scrim only. Through which the *intrépide* reader is trying to see.

"But denouement? There must be a denouement. Who will read a story with neither *une intrigue* nor *un dénouement*?" I tell her it is not for anyone to read, but only for me to write.

"But then who is the *intrépide* reader? *C'est vous?*"

I answer by saying the scrim is my computer screen, but as she does not have a computer I doubt she fully understands, even though she nods.

We are waiting for Monsieur to join us for dinner, and—perhaps—Mademoiselle, although the invitation by Madame has not been unconditionally accepted, something about getting to Bordeaux and back in search of art supplies. In the meantime, I sense that Madame is worrying about my *récit méditatif*—unlike when she was first amused.

From the stove where I am fixing the meal, I say that since there will be raveling, there will be unraveling. But when, and how, and by what means is yet for me to discover. However, "age will be necessary." She cannot help herself and smiles. "And some things will be left not said, nor explained," she says.

"*Ah oui,*" I say.

Montaigne

Monsieur once asked if I was married. I told him I had never married, but I was once asked. It was more intrigue than I intended to pass along. But he seemed not to have heard me.

He has finished filling my jug and Madame's as well. Outside it is raining: drip, drip, drip, as Dickens would write to earn his penny a word. It has been too warm in recent days to start the woodstoves for the few evenings that are damp and cold. I do, however, keep Madame's fireplace going. It cheers her, I think, to sit by it with Demain in her lap and Ginger toasting herself first on one side then the other.

"All was not to be merry as a marriage bell?" Monsieur says, his voice half a question. I am trying to guess if it is one of his quotations, or in response to what I had said. But before I can ask, he says: "Madame used to be married and now she is not: 'Hush! hark! a deep sound strikes like a rising knell!'" He is quiet for a moment.

"Byron," he says.

"And you?" I find myself having the nerve to ask. "Are you married?"

"There is a story I am," he says. He smiles the way he did when he used Madame's pet name. Then putting his arm around the side of the vat out of which he has just drawn the wine, he says: "Which wife is this? The one I adored first and so took a second, or the other the other way around?"

"Oscar Wilde," I say. Monsieur looks at me for a moment as if to drop a mask. Then he says: "When I was a boy, I worked in the Montaigne vineyards. One day the owner gave me a book of quotations in English that a guest had given him. I think he knew I wanted to learn the language. Before that, I had no English. Each night when I came home, I would study the book. I set myself a goal to learn three quotations a day and say them out loud as I was working in the vineyards. It was later that I would get the meanings. After I understood what I was saying, I would only learn the quotations I liked. Working the vines I talked to myself, and after a while I would have one of me say a quotation to the other of me, and the second me would answer in a quotation. For two years I did this. It was before I left for California."

I realize Monsieur has answered a question I did not ask, and not answered the one I did. I am charmed by this evasion, if that is what it is—and it is probably not. From a bin behind the vat he fetches a bottle, checks its cork and its punt, which I can see is deep. It has no label.

"Here," he says. "There is a *histoire* in this wine. It is yours for the drinking and telling." Looking at the bottle, I say that we are of an age when old wood is best to burn, old authors best to read, and old wine best to drink.

"I don't know it," he says. "But now I do. I assign it to Montaigne."

Today I Told a White Lie That Helped

Madame is getting restless. Over the years she has been the epitome of independence and it vexes her not to be so now. The doctor says she will be walking on her own in a few weeks (it has been more than a month since she fell), but she doesn't quite believe it. Monsieur R. tells her Virgil says we do the most damage to ourselves by impatience.

"I don't think he ever gets any of them right, and I wonder if once upon a time he knew better and just set about to test and tease me, but by now he has forgotten that was his purpose, and has it in his head as fact that it was Virgil. And that you said, 'Never trust the writer; trust the tale.'" I smile and she knows I said no such thing. But I think it is true.

"He is Google itself," she says.

I ask how she knows about Google—as I don't know much about it, only that it exists. She says the same, then adds: "I understand you can find what you want to know in an 'instant,' and that seems to me a dreary way to go about the life of the mind, as if knowing something in an 'instant' will lead to knowledge, much less to wisdom. Where is the pleasure of serendipity? And of friends who read as we do. I don't drink instant coffee. I don't make instant tea. Or Minute rice. I make *soupe éternelle*. There is more than a difference."

She seems gloomy at the thought of Google. I have been teasing her about one thing or another in the past few days to bring her cheer, but that is wearing thin. She knows her flowers are starting up and the garden needs tending. We all help as we can, but not much will lift her spirits until she can get around by herself.

Today I tell a white lie that helped. I said the fishmonger at the Monday market had asked after her; she likes the fishmonger, a broad-faced, large-shouldered man who juggles lemons at his stand in between customers. In fact it had been the flat-nosed egg woman (whom she doesn't like). Anyway, what's a fib good for, if not to bring on a smile? At the ranch where I worked, they were called "right lies," some mishearing passed down through the generations.

"Tell the fishmonger," says Madame, "that I will return when I can walk on my own through the market, and that we shall have champagne and snails for lunch at the Hôtel des Voyageurs to celebrate. He will be charmed to know we can turn *boudin noir* and *vin de table* into escargot and champagne."

"As will Monsieur R.," I say.

"It is where I got the menu," she says. "Only he claims such a menu is there, and after we have not had it, we will have had it. I know this to be true in advance of it being so."

Now, I am the one who smiles.

Someone is at Madame's door. But before I answer it for her, I ask: "Did you ever meet Mademoiselle's mother?" It is a question that I have been too shy to ask.

"Once, at the Monday market," she says. "She was not well, as I had been told. Bruno, that was her husband's name, was with her, as was their child. The next summer they did not come, and I think it was not long afterward that I learned from the people at the Château de Montagne that she had died. Of what, no one knew. I never got her name. Only Bruno's."

"And you have not asked Mademoiselle about her mother?"

"I thought it best she tell me herself if she wanted to," says Madame. "Maybe you should ask her, as you seem curious. That could be her at the door."

A Vignette in Place of a Dénouement

If I stay in this country, will I stir fiction into fact? Have others say for me what I cannot say so well for myself? Will soupe *éternelle be the life of my mind, and intrigue find me—but not in an instant? Or has it?*

Will blood sausage and table wine become snails and champagne one Monday in a ticket restaurant with a parrot that does not like me? Will large dogs toast themselves first on one side then the other in a fireplace with no gun over it? Will summer come and with it my histoire*? Has it already had both raveling and unraveling?*

Or is the story in Monsieur's wine bottle that I return to a recovered vision of Black-and-White Kansas, where moss is only on the north side of trees and rocks? Where we build fences with good wire, and stout corrals with strong gates. Where we feed the dogs first, and know why we set dead men.

Looking at the great sweep of pastures and horizons that stretch to the edge of the earth in all directions, will I believe it myself?

Qu'en sais-je?

Where I Am Now

The last of the tanned hides are still on the south wall of my cabin. There are rabbits. Sleeping over in my cabin I heard the owls. It is late summer. The Thin Man Window is open. My second morning I go through it and down the ladder.

Mencken Cody has stopped by to see who is here. He tells me he took the horses before the bank could get them. Charlene dropped a foal, a mare he named for Buck's wife. Angel is with the hippies on the Saline but cannot be ridden; Mencken has my saddle and Buck's as well. He knows to leave me be, and heads for Blaze.

Volunteer tomatoes have come up in Patsy's garden among the weeds. Milky, I think. The ranch is in some kind of legal limbo; the grass looks good, and with no cattle or horses, it is thick and high. I walk the shelterbelt to where Patsy and I buried Amos and Murphy. Gone is not gone, and because the door to my cabin blew open he has *un peu* of my domestic history.

I walk over to the cut where we stood that winter day looking north. *How much snow? Ten to twenty with wind.*

I go into the Home-House and sit at the Scar Table and remember for all of us: *I can come back to get you. She's not that kind of painter. Sing! Jesus-God. Good thinking. Demonically 13:23. Here, over here. She's not expected to live or die. I only play upright E-flat altos. 'To the greater woman of the ranch, from the lesser one.' Art is long, life is short.*

Following the line of the scar from one end to the other, I do not blink. Instead, my mind's eye makes intrepid paintings: Buck in the moonlight on Canyon Snip. Monique swimming. The heifers that first morning of the snow. A turtle head snapping in the dust of the yard. Me with Buck one day on horseback when he asked what it felt like to miss Monique—and after what I said, nothing more was said. Nor can I write it now.

The visions fray at the edges and fade in the background: Moshe taking himself into the pasture. The butane star coming on. Buck and Ellen walking together on a summer's night, looking for a bullwhip.

I write on the glass-topped table in my cabin with pictures and your postcard (script side up) underneath. An empty wine bottle is behind the scrim of my computer screen. Ghost cattle are waiting for spring. Prairie fires are ever-present. Jesus-God is in the air.

What comes around, comes around.

This *histoire* is what has become for "Even losing you, the alto voice I love..."

There is nothing more to write.

Acknowledgments

The author is pleased to acknowledge the help of his literary colleagues in their support of his work: James Dissette, Kathy Streckfus, Kaite Stover, Andre and Monique Kamala, Lisa Stewart, John Harris, and Kathleen Jones.

Robert Day

Robert Day's novel *The Last Cattle Drive* was a Book-of-the-Month Club selection. His short fiction has won a number of awards and citations, including two Seaton Prizes, a Pen Faulkner/NEA prize, and Best American Short Story and Pushcart citations. His fiction has been published by *Tri-Quarterly, Black Warrior Review, Kansas Quarterly, North Dakota Quarterly, Summerset Review,* and *New Letters* among other belles-lettres magazines. He is the author of two novellas *In My Stead,* and *The Four Wheel Drive Quartet,* as well as three collections of short fiction: *Speaking French in Kansas, Where I Am Now,* and *The Billion Dollar Dream.*

His nonfiction has been published in the *Washington Post Magazine, Smithsonian Magazine, Forbes FYI, Modern Maturity, World Literature Today, American Scholar,* and *Numero Cinq.* As a member of the Prairie Writers Circle, his essays have been reprinted in numerous newspapers and journals nationwide, and on such Internet sites as *Counterpunch* and *Arts and Letters Daily.* Recent book publications include *We Should Have Come By Water* (poems), *The Committee to Save the World* (literary nonfiction), and *Chance Encounters of a Literary Kind* (memoirs). Other publications include the novel *Let Us Imagine Lost Love* and *Robert Day for President: an Embellished Campaign Autobiography.*

Among his awards and fellowships are a National Endowment for the Arts Creative Writing Fellowship, Yaddo and McDowell Fellowships, a Maryland Arts Council Award, and the Edgar Wolfe Award for distinguished fiction. His teaching positions include Tthe Iowa Writers Workshop; the University of Kansas; and the Graduate Faculty at Montaigne College, the University of Bordeaux.

He is past president of the Associated Writing Programs; the founder and former director of the Rose O'Neill Literary House; and founder and publisher of the Literary House Press at Washington College, Chestertown, Maryland.

CPSIA information can be obtained
at www.ICGtesting.com
Printed in the USA
JSHW022141120721
16851JS00006B/282